MEET
MR. WRIGHT

OMAR SCOTT

outskirtspress
DENVER, COLORADO

Meet Mr. Wright
v2.0 r1.1

Outskirts Press, Inc.
http://www.outskirtspress.com

ISBN: 978-1-4787-3127-6

Outskirts Press and the "OP" logo are trademarks belonging to Outskirts Press, Inc.

PRINTED IN THE UNITED STATES OF AMERICA

I want to dedicate this book to Robert Jones, Thomas Johnson, Otis Ford, Terry Stokes, and Kalita Thomas, gone but not forgotten.

ACKNOWLEDGMENTS

I want to first thank God for blessing me with the talent to write a book like this. To my father Louis Scott, who is always supportive and encouraging. To my mother Toni Johnson, who is the best mom that anyone could ask for. To my wife Joyce, they say behind every successful man, is a good woman, and nothing could be truer when it comes to you. To my grandma Willie Mae Ryles, who was instrumental in giving me the background and history to write such a story. To my daughter Stevonne, you'll always be my heart. To my good friend Chris Yancey, who supported my work from the very beginning, and has been my sounding board to bounce ideas off of. To my friend Krissy Johnson, one of my biggest supporters, she never misses an opportunity to promote me and my work. To my cousin Dash, who's been like a brother to me, you've always inspired me to chase my dreams. To my boy Ricky Hunter, the most positive and inspirational man I know. To my professor Laurie Grey, who helped me to find my true voice. To my writing workshop classmates, Brian, Tara, Siaura, and Mindy, thanks for creating an atmosphere where ideas could flourish. To my boy Don Chase, a true friend who always listens to my problems. To my friend Rachael, the most intelligent woman I know. To Carey Lofton and Ricky Jackson, two brothers that always keep me right spiritually. To my little brother Chris and my sister Naiema, I love you guys. To my family Beverly, Richard, David, Byron, Ciephon, Edie, Anthony, Leonard, Jaden, Blake, Desmond, Chase, Leslie, Michael, Nathan, Charlotte, Kiona, Troy and Rochelle I love you guys. To my Supreme Swing family, Terry Tucker, Rick Rose, Marcus Kelly, Theresa Collins, Sicily Mason, Chris Smith, Sharika Abdur-Rahman. James Johnson. Felicia Fortner, Stephaney Johnson, Tamika Tucker, Shaun Brockington. Can't forget Larry Johnson, John Dixon, Charles Derrough, Anjuan Evans, Troy Henderson, and Andre Bowman. To my wise barber Larry Jones and all the brothers at LJ's barbershop. Sorry if I forgot anybody. Finally to all my fans that have supported me, a very special thanks to you.

INTRODUCTION

In my first year at college, I took philosophy. Not because I was interested in being enlightened, but because my friends told me it was an easy class. My professor, Dr. Graham, was an extremely passionate man. He was always looking for new and innovative ways to stimulate our minds and encourage freethinking. Take, for instance, my first mid-term; he had us write our own obituary. It was part of the subject that he had been teaching most of the first semester called, "Forward thinking." So in typical fashion, I wrote down some generic things I thought would be interesting, I made sure that I used proper grammar and punctuation. When Dr. Graham handed out the graded papers, I expected no less than an A. To my surprise, the grade was a D. Stunned; I waited around until class was over hoping to get some kind of explanation. Upon confronting my professor about my grade, Dr. Graham told me something I would never forget. He said, "What you gave me was a well typed laundry list. This assignment was not about listing your accomplishments; it's about gaining some insight into who you are as a man, your impact on other people's lives, and what you contributed to society. Was the world a better place with you in it?

Ironically, now I sit at my desk years later with the daunting task of writing my own father's obituary. And while Dr. Graham's words resonate in my head, the thought of summing up my father's entire existence in one paragraph seems absurd to me. My father, Neil Wright, was an extremely complicated man, and I couldn't even begin to sum up his life in a few sentences. My father was feared by many, respected by even more, but truly loved by only a precious few. He was a good man who did many bad things. And before you judge him, I offer you the proverbial pair of shoes so that you can walk a mile in them, to know him like I did. All that I ask is that you open your mind. This is his story.

– Mathew Wright

The morning silence at my father's home was broken when his cell phone rang. His eyes popped opened as he looked over at my mother to find her cutting down trees with her snoring. After more than thirty years of marriage, he learned to deal with it. Rolling over, he quickly grabbed the phone to answer it before it could ring a third time and wake her.

"Hello," he murmured wiping his almond colored eyes. Glancing over at the clock, he saw it was one in the morning.

"Neil, it's Frito," he replied in a husky voice.

"You have any idea what time it is?"

"I know brother. I'm sorry, but this couldn't wait. We got a big, big problem with the shipment! And I haven't been able to get in touch with our friend with the slick hair."

"Shit! Ok," my father responded as he sat up in bed scratching his salt and pepper hair. "Give me an hour and I'll meet you at the warehouse."

"Sure thing," Frito replied keeping his conversation short. He knew not to say too much over the phone, no telling who's listing in on the other line, FBI, DEA, maybe ATF. Any of them would love to catch my old man saying something incriminating, something they could use to build a case against him. They've been on his tail since the seventies and still haven't caught him yet. My father was brilliant at sidestepping potential landmines and avoiding the law, a criminal mastermind that has never seen the inside of a jail cell. The old man was as slippery as a bar of wet soap.

Hanging up the phone, he went to his contact list, scrolled down, and called his bodyguard and driver, "Hey Earl."

"Yes sir."

"I need you to pick me up in an hour."

"I'm on it sir," Earl answered sharply.

Sliding his feet into his slippers, my father rose to his feet, casually strolled over to the window, and peeked through the wooden blinds. The view from his penthouse apartment was magnificent. The hazy gray skies that covered the beautiful city of Dallas poured down rain in buckets for the past few days, with no end in sight. Walking into the bathroom, he stood over the sink and looked at his reflection for a moment. The years had been kind to him, despite the stressful position he held. The combination of his honey brown skin and age defining wrinkles made him look distinguishing and debonair.

Something that many of his friends who shared his age couldn't say. Twirling the hairs of his thick goatee, he pulled a small pair of scissors from the drawer and trimmed the gray hairs that were starting to grow out of control. Although it was late, my father was a stickler for dressing sharp, so he put on his favorite navy blue suit and burgundy tie that I bought him for father's day. Fully dressed, he leaned over and tenderly kissed my mother on the forehead before darting out the door.

By the time my father grabbed his coat and hat, Earl was pulling up in a black Lincoln town car. Earl was a former linebacker in college before blowing out his knee in the final football game of the season. A torn ACL I think. Anyway, the knee gave him problems ever since, caused him to limp noticeably. It didn't matter though, because when my father called, limp or no limp, he snapped to it. Earl hopped his big ass out of the car, popped open his umbrella, and briskly made it to the rear door to open it just as the concierge opened the building door for my father. Earl knew that the old man never called him out this late at night unless it was extremely serious, So Earl was on high alert. Unzipping his leather jacket to reveal the chrome forty-five tucked in his waistband, he surveyed the street for any sort of trouble.

"Hello boss," Earl uttered in his baritone voice as he shielded him from the drizzling rain with his umbrella.

"Earl," he replied slipping into the backseat, "We're heading to the old warehouse on Overton," he commanded reaching into his breast pocket and pulling out a cigar. Clipping off the butt before lighting it, he kicked back and relaxed in the leather seat while taking a nice long drag off the Cohiba.

With the freeway being so slick and the lateness of the hour, Earl cautiously navigated his way through downtown. The lights from the skyline led their way as they crossed the bridge into South Dallas. Passing by countless rundown factories, junkyards, and vacant buildings, they made their way into the heart of the industrial part of town. Earl checked the rearview mirror one last time to make sure they weren't followed before turning into the warehouse. The street and parking lot were desolate as they pulled up to the old shabby looking building. The area was dimly lit; most of the light fixtures in the parking lot or alongside the building were burnt out. The headlights of the car focused in on Frito. Frito, an enormous light-skinned brother with freckles, stood alone next to his black Cadillac Escalade with a cigarette dangling from his mouth, and shivering from the night air. At first sight, Frito resembled a big ole loveable teddy bear that you just want to give a gigantic hug. A guy who looked like a perfect fit to play Santa Claus during the holiday season, bouncing your sniffling little brat on his knee, while asking what they want for Christmas. But like the old saying goes, you can't judge a book by its cover. Frito was my father's right hand man, as ruthless as they come, and nigga who was tougher than a five dollar steak. Earl pulled up next to him and once again hopped out, popped open the umbrella, and opened the car door for my old man. Rising to his feet, my father walked over to Frito with Earl trailing close behind, shielding him from the rain.

"Sorry to get you out of bed my friend," Frito said with a stoic look wrapping his arm around my father's shoulder, "But I thought the situation needed your immediate attention."

"What do we got?" the old man responded.

"Follow me," Frito said as he turned and led the way. They walked over to the side of the building where several trailers were located. As they made their way around the back of one of them, Frito took off a pad lock, opened the back door, and grabbed a wooden case. "Take a look at this," he said as he handed the old man a machine gun. Reaching into his pocket, Frito pulled out a small flashlight and shinned it on the gun so my father could see it better.

"What's the problem?" he asked examining it from all angles.

"Crack it open."

My father opened it up, looked inside, and let out a subtle groan, "No firing pin! All of them?"

"Yeah, and I still haven't been able to get a hold of Pete, or any of his guys!" Frito replied taking another hit off his cigarette, "And we got several stores waiting on the merchandise, which we promised to deliver in the morning."

"I know, I know. Damn! And this is not like Pete. Something is not right. Let me think," he replied handing the gun back to Frito and rubbing his chin. Just then, they heard the remote sound of footsteps against the loose gravel near one of the other trailers in the distance. The noise caused all three men to whip their heads around simultaneously. Earl reached into his waistband and pulled out his heat.

"What the hell was that?" my old man asked.

"Wait here, I'll check it out," Frito said pulling out the nine-millimeter that was tucked in the small of his back and flashing the light in the direction of the sound. A shadowy figure zipped by him and into the darkness. Tiptoeing over to that direction, Frito followed the figure into the pitch-black night. Then, there was a loud noise followed by gunshots. Someone let out a grunt like they'd been shot, but Earl or my father couldn't tell if it's Frito or not.

"Frito, Frito!" my father yelled, but he didn't answer.

"Get behind me boss!" Earl commanded, as he stepped in front of my father and aimed his pistol in the direction of the sound. Then, the sound of another set of footsteps were running from behind them. "It's an ambush!" Earl yelled. Blinded by the darkness, he squeezed his trigger and began firing in any direction that he heard a sound come from, "Get to the car!"

My father turned and ran as fast and as low to the ground as he could with Earl behind him continuously squeezing off rounds. They made it back to the Lincoln as the bullets whizzed over their heads, shattered the windows, and ricocheted off the car and concrete. Carefully, they hustled to get the car doors open and slid inside. As soon as Earl climbed into his seat, he cranked the car, looked back to see if the old man was safely inside, and peeled out at top speed.

"You ok boss?" he asked looking in the rear-view mirror making sure the coast was clear.

My father reached into his coat and patted himself vigorously. The adrenaline was flowing and the only thought running through his mind was getting away. He relaxed for a second until he looked at his hand and noticed the blood dripping from it. At first, he thought it might have been from the broken glass in the seats. Then he started having trouble breathing. Ripping his shirt open, he saw the bullet wounds in his chest, "Shit, I've been hit," he yelled.

"Don't worry boss. I'll get you to the hospital!" Earl shouted, as he swerved around corners and ran through red lights until he got him to the emergency room.

Earl busted threw the double doors of St. Luke's hospital, forcefully grabbed the first person he saw in a pair of scrubs, and dragged him back to the car, "I got a man who's been shot!" he bluntly stated, as he flung the door open and carefully helped my father out the car.

When the hospital staff saw the seriousness of his injuries, they scrambled a team together and rushed him to the trauma room. Meanwhile, Earl calmly strolled over to an isolated corner and called me from his cell phone.

"Hello," I answered, half sleep.

"Matt, you better get to the hospital. Your father has been shot."

Things had begun to quiet down at St. Luke's Hospital. Earlier, the place had been crawling with detectives, reporters, and nosey ass people trying to get any information they could about my father's condition. It was a mad house! Now that visiting hours were finally over, all those people were forced to clear out. Even most of the nurses and doctors, which had been constantly walking the halls all evening, were rapidly decreasing before my tear-stained eyes. Of course, those rules didn't apply to us, because of my father's clout, condition, and the possibility that his life could still be in danger. It was the third night that my father, Neil Wright, had been in intensive care holding on for dear life after suffering several gunshot wounds. The doctors weren't optimistic about his condition. Therefore, my mother and I took turns staying with him constantly so that he would never be alone, and tonight was my turn.

I got up and stretched my legs for the first time in hours. They fell asleep from sitting in the same awkward position all day long. I had been sitting in the chair across from my father staring at the machine that made that eerie beeping sound while monitoring my father's vital signs. Walking over to the cabinet that was next to the door, I grabbed a blanket and prepared to make myself as comfortable as one could who has to sleep in a rock-hard chair.

I stuck my head out of the door to see that the hallways were now completely desolate. Other than the one nurse sitting at the monitoring station, everyone else seemed to have left. That is except for Earl and Bruce, my father's two bodyguards. Usually they took turns guarding him, but under the present circumstances, I thought the extra security was necessary. They stood on either side of my father's hospital room door. Two of my father's most loyal and trusted men, they never talked, they never moved. They just stood there watching every move like the royal guards in England dressed in red with the funny looking black hats.

"You fellows need anything before I crash?" I asked as my eyes darted back and forth between both guys.

"No Sir, we'll be fine," both men said in unison sounding like a pair of Siamese twins.

Shrugging my shoulders, I sat my blanket and sheet on the chair and walked over next to my father. He was lying there so peaceful. I gently stroked his thin salt and pepper hair. For an old man who had just been shot, he looked good. His honey brown skin was still full of life, and earlier that morning my mother had given him a shave. She knew how he was about his appearance. My father was not a vein man, but he was a neat one. And he liked his goatee to be neatly trimmed daily.

I went back over to the chair and started unfolding the sheets. Getting as comfortable as I could, I turned on the TV to catch the evening news and curled up under the blanket. Out the corner of my eye, I saw someone approaching. It looked like one of the nurses was checking in on my father again. She was dressed in all white like a typical nurse, but this woman was carrying a small black bag that caught my attention, and the attention of Earl and Bruce at the door. As she attempted to walk through the door, Bruce stuck out his arm and asked in a mincing voice, "Who are you, and what do you want here?"

"I'm a nun, young man. The Chaplin is on vacation, and I'm filling in for him," she replied pleasantly, despite Bruce's rudeness. It seemed odd to me, but this was a Catholic hospital.

"What's in that bag?" Bruce inquired further with his arm still blocking the doorway. Extremely overprotective when it came to my father, he wasn't taking any chances. To him, a woman could be just as treacherous as any man. For all he knew, this woman could be packing some heat in that bag looking for any opportunity to finish the job my dad's enemies started a few days earlier.

She slowly unzipped the black bag and pulled out a King James Bible and a small bottle of holy water. Bruce grabbed the bottle, took off the top, and held it to his nose.

"It's okay Bruce. You can come in ma'am," I interjected.

Bruce turned around and looked at me, nodded his head, and finally lowered his massive arms. With a polite smile, she took back her bottle from Bruce and casually strolled into the room. A small black woman, her head was covered with a white veil that matched her all white uniform. Looking at the small part of her face that wasn't covered, something about her caramel colored skin, her hazel eyes, and her lips seemed familiar. Even her very presence appeared to brighten the room as if God had walked in with her.

"Sorry about that, Sister. My father's life is in danger. We can't be too careful," I said as I offered my hand, "My name is Mathew, and you are?"

"Sister Simmons," she answered shaking my hand.

"Isn't it kind of late for you to be coming around?"

"Actually...no, not when we have a patient who requires immediate attention. I do apologize for the intrusion. We generally like to go around and pray with the sick when the family is not present so that we don't interrupt your short time together. But I was told by the nursing staff a few minutes ago that your father's condition was not good. He might not it make through the night. So I wanted to come down as soon as I could to pray with him and offer him a chance at salvation if he needs it."

"I see...well, he's all yours," I replied stepping back.

"Thank you." She knelt down beside the bed, closed her eyes, and began to pray silently. Rising back to her feet, Sister Simmons cracked opened that old Bible of hers and took the top off the holy water. She dabbed her thumb with holy water and touch my father on the forehead while saying, "In the name of the father, the son, and the holy spirit."

As she moved down his chest to make the sign of the cross over his body, my father suddenly opened his eyes. With catlike reflexes, he grabbed Sister Simmons's wrist tightly and blurted out, "What the hell are you doing?"

I hopped out of my chair and rushed over, "It's okay Pop. She's just praying for you," I blurted out lightly touching him on the shoulder. Turning toward me, he took a deep breath; I could tell his eyes were trying to focus. He was in and out of consciousness since his operation three days ago. Upon realizing that it was me standing over him, he smiled and slowly released her hand. "I'm sorry," he murmured.

"It's okay. If I woke up and saw a stranger standing over me, my reaction would probably be the same," she politely responded while smiling.

I bent over and kissed him on the forehead, "How are you feeling, Pop?"

"I've been better Matt," Then he tried to sit up again, "What happened to Frito?"

"We don't know yet. Nobody can find him. We're still trying to piece together what happened. Some of your best people are already on it," I whispered leaning close trying to show some discretion with the nun in the room.

"Where's your mom?"

"She went home a couple of hours ago to try to get some sleep. We've been taking turns staying with you over night, and tonight was my turn. It doesn't matter though, mom usually comes right back after a couple of hours anyway. I'll call her."

"Let her sleep. She deserves some rest."

"I gotta call her Pop. She made me promise to call if your condition changed at all," I stated as I patted my pockets for my cell phone, "Damn!

I must have left it in the car." I turned toward Sister Simmons, "Can you stay here with my father while I run to the car to get my phone?"

"Sure, no problem," she responded.

As I left the room, Sister Simmons turned her attention back to my father. She knelt down to pick up her Bible and bottle of holy water that she dropped on the floor when my father reached for her hand. "I'm sorry about that again...here, let me help," My father offered trying to sit up in the bed and help her out like the true gentleman he was.

"No, please lie down," she said putting her hand on his chest to keep him from sitting all the way up. "Save your strength."

Closing his eyes, my father took a deep breath and laid his head back down on his pillow. Still incredibly weak, it took every little bit of strength he had just to sit up. Readjusting himself in the bed to get more comfortable, my father turned toward Sister Simmons, "So...you're a nun?"

"Yes," she said putting her belongings on the table next to the TV.

"So are you a nurse too?"

She chuckled, "Of course not."

"So why are you dressed like one?"

She looked down at her outfit, "This is not a nurse's uniform. This is called a habit. It's just white because I work in a hospital."

"Oh…if you're only a nun, why are you working for a hospital?"

"Well, this is St. Luke, a Catholic hospital, and all Catholic hospitals have nuns. The Archdiocese believes in healing the soul as well as the body."

"Ah huh, you have to forgive me, Sister; I haven't spent much time in church over the years."

"It's quite alright sweetie. I'm not here to judge. I'm here to pray for you."

"You're about thirty years too late."

"It's never too late. We believe every soul is worth saving."

"Not mine. I'm under no illusions, Sister. I'm going to hell for the things I've done," my father replied as he looked over at the machine that was monitoring his vital signs, "It's only a matter of time."

"There is always forgiveness for those who ask for it. That's why God sacrificed his only son, Jesus. He died on the cross to save us from our sins. God loves you, and he'll forgive you, if you ask him."

"I don't think so, Sister. There's no place in heaven for a man like me. Do you have any idea who I am?"

Sister Simmons moved closer. She took my father's hand and looked deep into his eyes,

"You're a child of God, that's who you are. A child of God who strayed off the path and lost your way, but I can help you back, if you let me."

My father laughed, "A child of God. More like a stepchild of God. Shit, God turned his back on me a long time ago, Sister. He couldn't stand to watch the kind of man I've become, and I don't blame him."

"Don't say that. Believe it or not, God still loves you. Take, for example, the story of the penitent thief. You ever study that story in Sunday school when you were a kid?"

"No...I don't think so."

"It's the story of Dismas. You see, when they crucified Jesus; they also crucified two thieves on both sides of him. One of the thieves was an evil man who mocked Jesus, but the other thief. A man named Dismas, scolded the evil man for his lack of respect for Jesus. He said that they deserved to die for their evil deeds, and that Jesus did nothing wrong. Then he turned toward Jesus and asked Him to remember him in His Kingdom and Jesus said he would be in Paradise with Him."

"Hmm," my father mumbled under his breath.

"You see God is our heavenly father, and he sees us as his children. And just like all children, we make mistakes. I'm sure that handsome young son of yours has made a few over the years. But if he came to you and said he was sorry, wouldn't you still love him?"

My father fought to hold back the tears as he nodded his head in agreement.

"That's all God wants you to do. To believe in him, confess your sins, and just like Dismas; you too can have absolution," she said making one last desperate plea. She held his hand tightly and fell to her knees.

My father was astonished at her persistence. Other than his immediate family, nobody had shown that much concern for his life, for his soul. As much as he tried to fight it, he was touched. Sitting up in the bed, he motioned for Sister Simmons to signal one of the guards. "Earl, close the door, me and the Sister here need a few minutes alone. Tell my son to wait outside until we're finished."

"Yes sir," Earl responded accepting his orders without question. Earl stepped out and closed the door behind him.

My father turned his attention back toward Sister Simmons, "You mind if I ask you a question, Sister?"

"No."

"Why do you care so much about me? I mean you're so persistent and you speak with such passion. I just wonder what made you the way that you are. What drove you to become a nun?"

"I wanted to serve God, and what better way than to save souls."

"That's a pretty generic answer, Sister. I mean you could have served God as a regular woman. So why be a nun? Why give up the prospect of getting married and having children?"

"Well, like you, like Dismas; I have a past too. I did a lot of things I'm not proud of. I lived a sinful life at one time, and for me, becoming a nun was my way out. It gave my life purpose. It gave me a chance to give back and think of others first. That's why I can tell you, beyond a shadow of a doubt, that God does forgive. I'm a living testament to it."

"You're not bullshitting me, are you, Sister? You really believe I'm worth saving?"

"Yes, I do."

"If I'm going to do this, if I'm going to confess to everything, then I should tell you my whole story. I should start from the very beginning, or at least the beginning of where things started to go wrong."

"I understand."

There was a long pause as my father laid there staring up at the ceiling for a moment. Scratching the back of his head, he cleared his throat and locked eyes with Sister Simmons, "Okay…okay. What do I got to lose? I'm going to die anyway. You better have a seat Sister…this could take awhile."

I was twelve years old. Just an average kid at that age, matter of fact that was one of the things that really irritated me the most growing up, being average. I remember all my buddies who had these cool nicknames that reflected their personalities or appearances like Shorty, Peanut, Slim, and Pinball. But I never had a cool nickname because I was just so damn average. Average height, average build, average face, hell, even my damn dick was average. Nothing about me stood out at all. And up until that point, my life was average too. That is until I came home from my summer vacation.

It was a turbulent time. America was in complete chaos. The war in Vietnam was reaching its peak. Dr. King and Robert Kennedy were assassinated. Riots in every major city dominated the evening news on a nightly basis. Not even the Olympics were immune. Tommie Smith and John Carlos were taking heat for raising a gloved fist during the playing of the National Anthem. But for me, all those things were the least of my concerns. I was just a kid who couldn't wait to get home from my summer vacation and hang out with my buddies.

Every summer, since I was old enough, I spent with a family that belonged to the Fresh Air Fund. A summer program sponsored by the Herald Tribune, the Fresh Air Fund was supposed to take poor little black kids from the ghetto and link them with a family in the country. It was the city's feeble attempt at integration. Personally, I think it was a way to get all those bad ass kids out of the city for the summer. Crime goes down, and the parents get a two-month break from their kids without paying a dime, beautiful isn't it. Anyway, this summer I spent with Mr. and Mrs. Jenson. They were a sweet old white couple that had this beautiful horse ranch in Northern Pennsylvania where they breed Clydesdales. Usually, there were about a dozen of us kids, bad as shit, but uncharacteristically on their best behavior. That's because they knew that if those white folks reported their ass, they'd be kicked out of the program. Despite all that, it was fun. We got to feed and ride the horses during the day, and at night, we could run free and play all night long without a curfew. I loved it, because when I was at home my Momma wanted me in at dusk, no exceptions!

The train ride home that summer felt longer than usual. I was sweet on Pattie Mae Franklin, who lived in my same building. We both went to school at PS-1. That's right, the same school that the Heavy Weight Champ Floyd Patterson went to. Pattie Mae was so cute, and on the last day of school, she slipped me a note asking to be my girlfriend. Of course, I answered yes, but before we could hang out, I was on my way to Pennsylvania. I didn't even get the chance to get my first kiss yet. From my window seat, I was on the edge of my chair the entire way. When the Manhattan skyline and the Hudson River came into view, my chaperone, Ms. Armstrong, had to tell me to sit down a million times because I was so impatient. As much as I had fun on that ranch, I couldn't wait to get home. Pennsylvania is nice, but there was no place in the world like New York City, plus my girl Pattie Mae was there too.

As we pulled into Penn Station, I bolted from my seat, grabbed my duffle bag, and sprinted to the door. As soon as they opened, I could see my old man standing on the platform. I was worried that my Pop wouldn't recognize me. My natural had grown out, and I was in bad need of a haircut. I was dressed in my favorite pair of dungarees and a new Steelers football jersey that the Jenson's bought me as a gift. Since Pop was a diehard New York Jets fan, my jersey was sure to piss him off.

My father was cool as shit. He didn't walk; he strolled, like a man with incredible confidence and swagger. His dark skin was smooth like chocolate. He had a cold-blooded gray fedora that he wore broken down in the front like Duke Ellington. A snappy dresser too, his slender frame was wearing a brown silk shirt and a freshly starch pair of slacks that fit him perfectly. He was clean-shaven, except for the small piece of hair that he wore over his pointed chin. Carrying a bag under his arm, he pulled off his dark shades to scan the station for me. Once he spotted me running over to him, he flashed a smooth grin and opened his arms to hug me, "What's happening kiddo?" he asked.

"Hey Pop," I responded squeezing him tightly.

"Your acting like you missed me kiddo."

I quickly released him and stood back. "A little, I'm just glad to be home," I said playing it off trying to be cool. Truth is I missed him greatly. He was my hero. I tried to pattern myself after him, but I would never tell him that. My father was a *man's man*. He's from the old school, when fathers didn't show affection, didn't kiss their sons, and didn't walk around saying I love you at the drop of a hat. Silly macho nonsense I know, but in those days, that's just how it was. Fathers and sons didn't cross that unsaid boundary.

"I got a surprise for you. Something you've been wanting for awhile," he said patting the paper bag he was carrying.

"What is it?" I asked almost giddy.

"You'll have to wait until we get back to the house."

"C'mon Pop."

"Just wait until we get back home, I want your mom to see too."

"Okay."

We went down stairs to catch the subway home. We didn't have a car, matter of fact, Pop didn't even have a driver's license. If we needed to go anywhere, we went by subway or occasionally, by cab. Of course, like the average black family in the sixties, we lived in the projects, the Governor Alfred Smith Housing project to be exact. However, we were fortunate; the Smith projects were the model projects for all of New York City. On Madison St. between Catherine St. and St. James Pl. downtown, the Smith Projects was spitting distance from city hall. Anytime there was a visitor to the city, Senators, Presidents, and dignitaries, the Man would show off our projects. Because of that, our building was one of the nicest well-kept buildings of any kind in Manhattan. You couldn't find graffiti or trash anywhere. If you called the super for a backed-up toilet, he was there the next day. They would even give you a ticket for walking on the immaculately kept grass.

We stepped out of the subway on a muggy Monday afternoon. I started sweating almost immediately. It was getting close to lunchtime, and the streets were flooded with people. There was way more people than normal because of all the construction that was going on. The city had closed off several streets that morning as workers were preparing to lift more metal beams to the top of the World Trade Center that was close to being done. Matter of fact, the first thing I saw coming out of the subway was the large cranes sitting on top of the two enormous buildings that dominated the Manhattan skyline. As we approached our building, I waived to my friends who were out front playing *stick-ball* in the street. Pop was in a rush to get home, so I couldn't stop and *shoot the shit* like I wanted to.

We made it home and took the elevator up to our modest two-bedroom apartment that was located on the 12th floor. It was small, but clean, our house always smelled like ammonia. Even though most of our furniture was secondhand, Momma did her best to spruce things up and add some style. She knitted a dark-brown quilt and placed it over the couch to cover up the fact that the fabric was worn out and torn. Momma also used an old white curtain that she found at a flea market in Brooklyn as a dining room tablecloth to hide the very old scratched up surface. Our walls in the living room and in the hallway were plastered with pictures. We didn't need a photo album because they were all on the wall. Momma loved pictures. It didn't matter what kind of picture it was or who was in it. If she thought it was cute, it was going up on the wall. She even hung up a naked baby picture of me covered in baby oil. For years, I had to endure the embarrassment of that picture until I made it mysteriously disappear. I got my ass tanned, but it was worth it.

Walking in, I could see my Momma in the kitchen sitting on a stool with a cigarette in one hand, and a glass of whiskey in the other. She had this somber look on her face when we came in. Her eyes were blood-shot red, and her jet-black shoulder-length hair was tied into a ponytail. Momma's grandmother was full-blooded Cherokee, so she had these strong Indian features like high cheekbones and thin lips. Things were a little testy between my parents before I left. Momma's parents, my grandpa and grandma, had been killed in a car wreck a year ago on their way up from South Carolina to see us. Momma took their deaths hard. Every day for the past year, up until the day I left, Momma would just sit at the window in her floral housecoat and house shoes, gazing up at the sky and drinking heavily.

"Hi Momma," I said dropping my bag at the door and running over to give her a hug and a kiss.

Momma looked like her smile was forced, as she kissed me on the forehead and quickly turned her attention back to cooking without acknowledging my Pop. From the delightful aroma that came trickling out of the kitchen, I could tell Momma was cooking my favorite dish, beef stew, and cornbread. She sat down her drink and with a large spoon in her hand began stirring the pot. "You behaved yourself at camp?" Momma asked taking another puff off her cigarette and then flicking her ashes into the ashtray on the counter.

"Of course Momma," I replied as I turned back around to see my father rolling his eyes at my Momma. "So Pop, you gonna give me that surprise now?"

"Sure," he answered grabbing the paper bag and opening it up, "Estelle, come see what I got Neil."

My Momma took another sip of her drink and then walked over with her hands on her hips waiting for my father to reveal what he'd bought. He turned toward me smiling as he opened the packaged, "I had to pull a few strings to get this before it was released in stores." He pulled out

Miles Davis' new album, *In a Silent Way,* and handed it to me.

"Wow!" I blurted out. I was a big time Miles Davis fan. I loved his music, still do. Miles was my second favorite musician after my Pop. My Pop was a trumpet player too. Pop had his own band called, the Wright Quartet that played for a small club up in Harlem. As I said, I wanted to be like my Pop, that included wanting to play the trumpet. I begged him until he finally broke down and decided to teach me the horn two years ago.

"Thanks Pop," I said grinning from ear to ear.

"Ray, I can't believe that you would buy an expensive record as bad as we're doing right now," Momma interjected angrily with her hands on her hips.

"C'mon, Estelle. I just wanted to do something nice for my boy."

"You wanna do something nice for him, how about getting him and me out of these damn projects."

"Do we have to get into this right now?"

My Momma looked at the clock on the wall and reached for her purse. She pulled out a quarter and handed it to me, "Jimmy will be coming by any minute. Run down stairs and put in my numbers for me while me and your father talk."

"Yes Momma. What numbers?"

"Triple twos, like always," she barked.

Reluctantly, I turned and left out of the door. I could feel my mother's eyes piercing the back of my head until I closed the door. I made it outside to the front stoop to see old Ms. Henry from the third floor that always had rollers in her hair and Mrs. Edwards from the tenth who smelled liked mothballs and had more hair on her upper lip then my old man.

"Hello Neil, just getting back from the *Fresh Air Fund*?" Ms. Henry asked sitting up in her chair.

"Yes ma'am."

"Where you go this time?"

"Pennsylvania," I said trying to keep the conversation short. Those two old ladies could ramble on for hours. "Have y'all seen Jimmy?"

"Need to put in the numbers for your Momma, huh?" Mrs. Edwards asked.

"Yeah."

"He just walked around the corner. If you run you can catch him," Ms. Henry answered.

I quickly waived to thank the ladies for their help and quickly sprinted around the building to catch up with Jimmy. Now Jimmy was a young Italian kid who ran numbers for the Bonanno crime family. The Bonannos ran the number rackets in lower Manhattan in the sixties, and Jimmy was one of their associates. Even though the lottery was illegal, it didn't matter because the Bonannos had most of the cops walking the beat in the neighbor on their payroll. I personally saw Jimmy taking bets right in front of the beat cops on more than one occasion.

"Jimmy!" I yelled out.

He stopped, slowly turned around, and waited for me to approach. "Hey Neil, your mom wants to play those triple twos again," he joked.

"Yeah," I said running up. I was hunched over trying to catch my breath as I pulled the quarter out of my pocket to give to him.

"All right," Jimmy replied as he signed a slip of paper for my confirmation, "No time for chit-chatting today Neil, I'm running behind," he said stuffing the money in his pocket and quickly taking off to finish his rounds. "Catch you later."

As I turned and walked back to the building, I heard that oh so sweet sound that every kid loves. Excited, I stood fully erect. My ears immediately perked up. With my head on a swivel, I scanned the area searching for where the sound was coming from like a bloodhound trying to pick up a scent. Then out of the corner of my eye, I spotted the white truck slowly turning into the parking lot across the street from our building. There he was, the ice cream man!

I wasn't the only one who heard the ice cream man coming, the rest of the kids playing outside were already sprinting toward our building yelling at the top of their lungs, "The ice cream man is coming! The ice cream man is coming!"

They all lined up on the sidewalk next to the building copying my momma's bit. See, momma came up with this sweet system, a sort of short cut to keep me from having to come up twelve floors. She'd grab a small brown paper bag, place the change she was going to give me inside, and then she put in a rock to keep it from blowing away. After twisting the bag shut, momma would lean out of the window and drop the bag down to me. I was always the first to get my ice cream. After the other mothers got wind of this, they started doing the same thing.

So there we were, a bunch of nappy-headed kids standing single file under the window waiting for our mothers to drop down a sack of change. As I waited for my turn in line, I saw an old white man in a Buick pulling into the parking lot. He pushed opened his car door with his foot while sliding out of his car lugging a heavy briefcase. Ms. Henry and Mrs. Edwards who were sitting on the stoop frantically started gathering their things together and rushing back into the building.

"Neil, you better get upstairs and tell your Momma that Mr. Buckman, the welfare man, is coming!" Ms. Henry urged.

I quickly hopped on the elevator and went back to our apartment. As I approached our apartment door, I could hear my Momma's voice in the hallway cussing and screaming. I hesitantly turned the knob to open the door. Sticking my head in first, Momma promptly turned her attention toward me. "I thought I told your ass to go downstairs while me and your father talk! See, this is the type of shit I'm talking about. Nobody around here listens to me!"

Pop was standing there with his hat pushed up wiping the sweat off his forehead with a handkerchief. He stepped in front of Momma and calmly said, "What do you need kiddo?"

"Mr. Buckman, the welfare man, is coming!" I announced.

Momma rolled her eyes and turned around in disgust. Pop quickly snapped to attention. "Is he coming this way?" Pop asked.

"I don't know."

"Okay, he could be coming here. We gotta hide everything. Neil, take all the toys out of your old toy box and put them in the closet. Quickly!" Pop commanded clapping his hands. "C'mon, Estelle. Help me hide this stuff. We can finish talking later."

"I don't give a damn! I'm tired of this shit, Ray. I'm tired of living like this," Momma yelled.

"You'll be living on the street if Buckman

comes in here and sees us living like this," Pop shot back.

You see in New York, back in the sixties, welfare was totally different than it is now. The city thought that in addition to giving you money, they could tell you how to live and what you could have. For instances, they thought that if you were poor enough to get welfare, you shouldn't be able to afford any luxuries, like a telephone, or a toaster, or even a stereo. And to help enforce these ridiculous policies, representatives were free to drop by your house at anytime for surprise inspections.

Momma just stood in the middle of living room with her arms folded tapping her foot staring at Pop. Pop didn't hesitate; he scrambled to the kitchen, began to unplug the phone and the toaster, and placed them in my toy box. He quickly went over to the closet and grabbed a large sheet. We had a brand-new television slash stereo console that my Momma bought when she hit the numbers a few months back. Pop closed the doors, threw the sheet over it, and put a plant on top to make it look like a table.

"C'mon Estelle, please," Pop begged.

Momma finally decided to help. She grabbed a large towel out of the closet, walked over to the kitchen table, pulled off the good silver, and rolled it up in the towel. Just as Momma placed the silverware in the toy box, we heard a knock at the door. We all froze in our tracks. Pop surveyed the apartment one last time to make sure nothing of worth was still out. He crept over to the front door and asked, "Who is it?"

"It's Mr. Buckman with the welfare department."

Pop slowly opened the door. Mr. Buckman stuck his head through the crack in the door, "Hello Mr. Wright, may I come in?"

"Sure, sure," Pop stammered as he wiped his sweaty palms on the back of his pants.

"I just stopped by to see how you folks are doing," Mr. Buckman said smiling as he walked in and started snooping around. Mr. Buckman was this fat old white man with a terrible looking comb over and a striped suit that looked like it was about two sizes too small. He sat his briefcase on the dining room table while he slyly roamed through the kitchen looking for anything out of place. "You folks have a very lovely home, nicely decorated, looks expensive," he commented touching on my Momma's nice linen tablecloth.

"I know you didn't come all the way up here to tell me you like my decorating," Momma snapped rolling her eyes at him. She couldn't stand him, or any of the welfare people they sent to our house. As far as she was concerned, what we did in our home was our business.

Mr. Buckman ignored her comment. He walked over to the stove. Leaning over the pot to look at the stew, he sniffed the aroma, "Beef stew for dinner? You folks are doing pretty well, huh?"

My old man was visibly nervous. He kept re-adjusting his hat and pacing back and forth while watching Mr. Buckman poke around our apartment. Momma walked over and got right in front of Mr. Buckman's face, "What the hell do you want?"

Mr. Buckman scrunched his face, "Is that alcohol I smell, Mr. Wright?"

"And what if is? Who the fuck are you, the police?"

"That's not a nice thing to say, Mrs. Wright."

"If you didn't like that, you damn sure ain't gonna like what I say next?"

"I'm just doing my job Mrs. Wright. Just doing my job," he said smiling as he walked into the living room. Strolling over to the console that my Pop threw the sheet over, he turned and commented, "Interesting table, mind if I have a look under the sheet?"

"Yes I mind! Matter of fact, I mind your ass being in my damn house. You crackers think you can come into anybodies home and walk around like you own the place," Momma yelled going into the kitchen to get her broom.

"Welfare recipients are supposed to submit to inspections, and that's all I'm doing," Mr. Buckman responded.

"Well, you've inspected. Now get your shit and get the hell out my house!" Momma said pointing her broom at his head.

"Mrs. Wright, please. I'm just trying to do my job," he said as he recoiled. The thought of my Momma going upside his head with that broom wiped that silly smirk off his face.

Momma showed him no mercy. She opened the door and chased him out of the house. I never saw an old white man move that fast. He tripped several times and even dropped some of his papers on his way out the door and down the hallway as Momma hit him in the feet with that broom. Mr. Buckman scurried down the hall, like a dog with his tail between his legs. I giggled, as Momma didn't take any shit off anyone.

A week had passed by and things seemed to be quieting down a little. Momma was still drinking daily, but she was keeping busy. Pop didn't like her to work, so she volunteered as a secretary for the NAACP who had a branch office in Harlem. She worked the phones, passed out leaflets, and kept the minutes for any meetings they had. On top of her normal duties, anytime there was a civil rights violation, anytime a black person wasn't allowed in a restaurant or café, anytime a brother couldn't get a job because of the color of their skin, she was there with her picket sign standing up for the cause, even if that meant getting arrested. That was one of the reasons I had to grow up so fast and contribute to the house, you know cooking and cleaning, getting myself ready for school. Momma really needed my support. Last year alone she was arrested a half dozen times. So, with Pop working at night and sleeping during the day, they had limited interaction during the week, but that all ended one faithful Saturday night.

It was around ten o'clock and Pop was getting concern. Dressed in his finest black suit, he had his gray fedora cocked back on his head while pacing back and forth waiting for my Momma to come home. Every five minutes he turned and looked at the clock on the wall and then turn toward me asking, "Where the hell is your mother?" Usually, he left to go to the work around eight in the evening. Pop would meet up with the band backstage at least two hours before a gig, so that they could warm up and discuss the play list before hitting the stage.

I was sitting on the couch in my pajamas with my belly full of corn beef and hash that Pop had fixed for dinner. Pop wasn't a terrible cook; he could whip up a nice little meal on the fly when Momma wasn't home. I was starting to doze off while watching Sammy Davis Jr. cut up on *Laugh-In*. It was a long day, and I could feel my eyelids getting heavy with each passing moment. Although Pop was always tired and sleep deprived from working late nights, he liked to spend Saturday afternoons together before he went to work. That day he took me to Coney Island where we hung out, rode a few rides, and got some franks from Nathan's.

Pop was growing more irritated as he moved closer to the window in hopes that he might see her approaching. Pulling his horn out of the case, he gently caressed it with a special cloth that he recently bought. My Pop's most prized possession in this world was his trumpet. I swear that horn was never further than arms reach from him. It was the first thing I saw him with in the morning, and the last thing he touched before going to sleep. He kept it spotless, wiping it down constantly and oiling it every night. Pop would handle his horn much like a gentlemen would handle a fine woman, with tenderness and care.

Finally, about ten, the key turning those old deadbolt locks woke me out of my sleep. The door creaked open and Momma came stumbling through holding a half-empty pint of gin. Pop was fuming as he sat his horn down and helped Momma over to the loveseat. Pop started to say something, but he turned and looked at me first. I kept my eyes closed pretending to be sleep.

"Where the hell have you been, Estelle? You know I was supposed to be uptown by now, my first set started at ten," Pop asked in disgust as he snatched the bottle of gin from her hands and sat it on the coffee table.

"What does it matter? What does anything matter anymore?" Momma slurred.

Pop took a deep breath, "Estelle, baby. I know what you're going through. I lost my parents too. I know it's hard, but you gotta shake out of this funk."

"I figured you'd say some shit like that, this being your fault and all."

"My fault?"

"Your fault! It's your fault that my parents drove to New York for a surprise visit. You acted as if you couldn't take a weekend off from that nickel a dime ass job of yours to go see my parents. You knew how much they missed me. You knew how much they wanted to see me. But you just kept putting it off. There was always an excuse why we couldn't visit them," Momma cried. "Now they're dead from some car wreck that could've been avoided."

"It was an accident baby, an accident. I'm sorry," he said trying to console her.

"You're sorry. You hear that mom, you hear that dad?" Momma screamed with her arms stretched out looking at the ceiling. "He's sorry. I gave up my life for you; I married you, left my family behind, and moved to New York so that you could live out this... pipedream of being a jazz musician, and the only thing I have to show for it is being a bastard-child that's broke."

"C'mon, baby. That's not fair. Now I know things haven't gone exactly like I planned."

"Things haven't gone as planned, that's an understatement Ray. We've been here thirteen years, and ain't shit changed. We have nothing! And now I don't even have my family anymore."

"You still have me. You still have Neil, and we love you."

"Ray… I can't stand to look at your face anymore. Do you realize that? I hate you. I hate this life. I hate this God forsaken city. I hate everything about it. The smell, the people, being on welfare, living in this project, the over crowed streets, I hate it all."

"Okay, you're drunk, Estelle. Why don't you go lay down, before you really say something you'll regret later?"

"The only thing I'll regret is staying here another minute. I'm outta here," Momma said storming into the bedroom and pulling out her suitcase. She slammed it on the bed, flung it open, and started throwing in all her clothes from the closet.

"Wait a minute, Estelle! Let's talk this over first," Pop pleaded standing in front of her and the suitcase.

Momma rolled her bloodshot eyes at Pop, "There's nothing more for us to talk about."

"Yes there is. What about Neil?"

"Neil is old enough to choose who he wants to be with," she said pushing Pop out of the way so that she could stuff more clothes in her bag.

"Choose…he needs both parents to be there for him."

"Well, that's not going to happen. So like I said, he can choose who he wants to live with."

"There is no choice woman! My son isn't going anywhere."

"Fine! I'll call him when I get settled," Momma said as she zipped up her suitcase and headed to the front door.

"So just like that, you're leaving. No goodbyes, no nothing?"

Momma opened the front door, turned around, and said, "Goodbye." I wanted to jump in and say something, but I was taught a long time ago not to get into grown folks conversations. That's how you get a backhand slap to the mouth. Besides, momma probably just needed a little time to calm down. She'll be back I thought.

CHAPTER 5

AUGUST 10, 1968

I woke up that next morning realizing that I fell asleep on the couch. The house felt strange, different, knowing that my mother was not there. I wasn't as close to Momma as I was to Pop, but I loved her all the same. I walked over to my Pop's room to find him sitting on the bed still dressed in the same suit he had on last night. He had a blank expression as he stared at the wall while fiddling with his trumpet. Out the corner of his eye, he saw my head peeking through the cracked door.

"Hey kiddo, come over here for second," Pop said in a cracked voice. "Have a seat."

"Yes sir."

I slowly walked over and sat down next to him. He pulled me closer and put his arm around my shoulder, "Your ah…your mom has been having some problems lately. She's going through some things right now…and ah; she's going to leave for a while. She still loves you, and she'll be back, but in the meantime, I'm really going to need your help around here. You're going to have to grow up and become a young man. I need you to be responsible and trustworthy like never before until she gets back. Can I count you, son?"

"Of course, Pop," I answered giving him a much-needed hug. I never bothered telling him that I overheard the whole fight. There was no need. "Anyway I can help, just let me know."

Momma was true to her word; she left that night and never returned. A couple of days later she called to check on how I was doing, but I could tell by her slurred words that she was still drinking heavily. At first, she would call every day, after about a month it was weekly, couple a more months passed, we didn't hear from her at all.

Pop was visibly shaken, but he never allowed Momma's departure to affect our daily routine, not even as the new school year started. He usually made it home from a gig about three in the morning. While I was still sleep, he would fix breakfast. Nothing too fancy, normally just eggs, toast, and some pan sausage. He would iron my clothes and set them out on the edge of my bed. Normally, I would do all this myself, but I think Pop was trying to stay busy and keep his mind occupied. Finally, he'd wake me up around six in the morning. By that time, Pop was dead tired. After I was dressed and finished eating, I'd poke my head in his room to find him crashed out on the bed. Sometimes he was so tired; he wouldn't even bother getting undressed first. When that happened, I'd pull his socks and shoes off, and tuck him in under the covers.

On Friday and Saturday nights, Pop would sometimes take me with him to the club. He didn't like to, but it was hard for him to find someone to watch me on a consistent basis, and he didn't want me sitting at home all night alone. He worked at *Charlie's*, which was uptown in Harlem on 125th St. and Lennox. It was hot jazz spot at the time, despite the rough neighborhood. I remember the first time I ever went there and saw my Pop's name on the marquee in bright lights, *The Wright Quartet*. It was so cool.

So about three months passed by since momma left when my old man decided to take me with him to *Charlie's* one Saturday night. It was September, and the temperature dropped so we both hand on light jackets that night. Pop called a Gipsy taxicab company that he used when going uptown. They always arrived on time right in front of our building. Besides having the lowest rates, they were one of the few cab companies that would even come to the projects or go uptown. Harlem was rough, and Pop was well dressed traveling with his most prized possession, his trumpet, so he would routinely take a cab to work, especially on the weekend. The

A-train uptown was quicker, but far too risky at night. Men dressed in suits, carry a case, were fair game to the young hoodlums that prowled the subway stations looking for their next mark.

The cab dropped us off in the alley behind the club where one of the club's bouncers, Chubb, was watching the back door. Usually, the other members of Pop's group were standing out back, smoking luck-strikes, and cutting up. But since the weather was chilly that night, Chubb was outside all alone.

"Evening Mr. Wright," Chubb said tipping his cap. The alley was dimly lit, and Chubb was so dark that the only thing you could make out about him was his massive smile. "I see you brought my main man with you. What's happing little Neil?" he said giving my Pop and me some skin.

"Hey," Pop and me shot back.

"Say Mr. Wright, can you do me solid and see Mr. Charlie. He says he wants to see you upstairs, as soon as possible."

"Cool. Are the rest of the fellows here yet?" Pop asked.

"Moe and Felix are backstage, but I haven't seen Danny yet," Chubb responded as he pounded on the rear steel door to signal the inside man. The old rusty door made this loud clicking sound before finally opening. Pop nodded at Chubb as

I followed him inside. Jaime, who was the boss's nephew, locked the door behind us. We walked down this drafty corridor made of brick until we got to a narrow wooden staircase that led upstairs to Charlie's office. Pop lightly tapped on his door.

"Who is it?" An old scruffy voice bellowed out.

"It's Ray, Chubb said you wanted to talk to me," Pop yelled through the thick door that separated us.

"Come on in."

Pop pushed the door open and saw Charlie, who stood up for a brief moment. The elderly white man looked old and decrepit. His eyes were sunken into his head and his skin was wrinkled and mushy like rubber. The old man motioned for us to come in as he removed the cigar from his mouth and started coughing uncontrollably. "Please, have a seat," he said pounding his chest before putting the cigar back in his mouth to take another drag, "You want a Tootsie roll, Neil?" he asked holding out a glass jar filled with them.

"Thank you sir," I replied helping myself to a handful.

"This is kind of personal Ray, you sure you want your boy in here for this," Charlie asked dumping his ashes in the bronze ashtray that sat on his cherry wood desk.

"It's okay. I like to keep him close to me," Pop

said with a confused look on his face. It was apparent that he wasn't quite sure where Charlie was going with this formal meeting. Just this morning, Pop was talking about how great things were going at the club while giving me my daily trumpet lessons. He even mentioned that he was thinking about adding a saxophonist to form a quintet.

"Ray, I'm gonna be frank with you, over the last couple of months...your performances have left something to be desired. You're constantly late. Your group's sound is getting old and stale, and you're not packing them in like you used to."

"I know I've been late. I'm sorry about that, Charlie. You see my wife left me, and I'm trying to take care of my son alone," Pop explained tilting his fedora back on his head.

"I understand Ray, but this is a business, and your problems are affecting my bottom line," Charlie interrupted coldly while taking another drag off his stinky cigar. "I think it's time to go in a different direction."

"Wait a minute Charlie, let's talk about this. It's me, Ray. I've been with you for years. I know that lately I've been a little bit off, but I can fix this. I promise I'll be on time from now on, and I've been working on some new stuff for the group. I was even telling my boy earlier that, I planned to add a sax player. That would definitely spice things up." Pop said scooting up on the edge of his seat.

"I'm sorry Ray, but I'm not convinced. We've had this discussion before about your music. There's been two more clubs that have opened in the last four months, and they're stealing my business. You're late and you're playing that old bee-bop style music. I want that fresh, new, hip sound that the young kids like," Charlie said snapping his wrinkled fingers, "And I need people who I can count on. I like to help you, but I'm not running a charity," Charlie stated then he paused for a second and took a deep breath, "I'm gonna have to let you go Ray."

Pop slowly stood up and leaned over Charlie's desk. "Please Charlie, don't do this. I need this gig. I can make this right. I can change my sound, just give me chance."

Charlie didn't bother looking up at my Pop as he begged for his job. He simply reached into his desk, pulled out a white envelope, and handed it to my Pop, "Here's one months' severance."

Pop stood there for a moment, in a daze. He bowed his head like a defeated man. It seemed like an eternity went by as Pop stood there looking at the white envelope in Charlie's extended wrinkled hand. It reminded me of the movie *Lady Sings the Blues* when Diana Ross looked at a folded twenty-dollar bill that Billy Dee Williams had in his hands, waiting on her to take it from him. I know my Pop; he didn't want to take that envelope. Pop was a man of tremendous pride. But unfortunately, in tough times, money is stronger than pride. Finally, he reluctantly took it.

After Pop took that envelope, Charlie leaned over and nodded. I turned around to see the normally smiling Chubb was now stoned faced. He walked over and in a very serious tone announced, "I think it's about time for you and your son to leave, Mr. Wright."

Chubb escorted us out of Charlie's office and down the stairs. Backstage, in one of the dressing rooms warming up, were Felix, Danny, and Moe. Felix, who had on a dark pair of shades, was my Pop's drummer. His drum solos were the thing of legend. Moe, a yellow brother with the coolest looking conk I had ever seen, was a whiz on the piano. And Danny, a weird-looking guy whose eyes seemed like they were too far apart, was the cello player. As we entered the dressing room, Pop closed his eyes and sighed. I could tell he was quickly thinking of a way to break the terrible news to the fellas.

"I need to talk to you guys for a minute," Pop said readjusting his hat on his head. The guys slowly gathered around him. "Boys, I got some bad news. I don't know how to tell you this. It seems like Charlie is cutting us loose."

Danny, Felix, and Moe started looking at each other strangely.

"Look…this is my fault. I know I've been off my game. But I don't want you to worry. I promise you guys; I will find us another gig. We'll be onstage before the end of the month, you'll see," Pop said smiling trying to reassure them.

Felix looked at Danny and Moe, stepped closer to my Pop, and put his hand on his shoulder, "We've already found a new gig, Ray."

"You have. That's great. Where's the new spot at?" Pop asked exuberantly rubbing his hands together.

Felix turned around and looked at Danny and Moe once again. "Ray…we're going to stay here."

"What the hell are you talking about man?"

Danny and Moe walked over and stood behind Felix for support, "We've been asked by the new guy who Charlie hired to join his band."

Pop's jaw fell open, "How could you?"

"We're sorry Ray," Danny added.

"Sorry, I gave you motherfuckers a chance when nobody else would, and this is how you repay me?" Pop snapped.

"C'mon, Ray. We got mouths to feed. We didn't want to, but what choice did we have. If you were in our shoes, you would do the same thing," Moe interjected.

Pop just shook his head in disgust, "I'm sorry

you feel that way." He grabbed my hand and led me out of the door. I learned an important lesson that night. When push comes to shove, money doesn't just trump pride, it trumps everything!

The few hundred dollars in that envelope didn't last us long, and consequently, things started getting tight. I mean really tight. Meat completely disappeared from our diets. Something simple as a ham sandwich or a frank was a rare treat. Pop was doing everything he could to stretch a dollar. Shit, a loaf of bread was damn near a quarter. And to add insult to injury, since Momma left, we stopped getting food stamps too. We had to tighten up our belts, literally.

Despite the bad fortunes, Pop kept his chin up. He refused to let these tribulations break his spirit. He kept a positive attitude. Every day, he would get dressed in his best black suit, put on a smile, and go to the local clubs, bars, and night spots looking for a new gig. Although Pop had great determination and supreme confidence, he struggled to find anything. The pickings were very slim, and since Pop was older and had trouble adapting to the new style of music, he had problems getting another gig. After a couple of months went by with no money coming in at all, things got so rough that Pop went out looking for any job he could find. His options were limited though. The only thing he knew how to do was play the trumpet. And nobody wanted to hire an older black man with no work history when they could hire a younger man who was willing to do the same job for less money.

Without any cash coming in, the bills started piling up. The tensest part of Pop's day was his trip to the mailbox. It was an event that he mentally had to prepare himself for. Before he went down to the first floor and check the mailbox, he'd sit at the kitchen table in silence, smoke two cigarettes, and have a shot of Momma's whiskey that she left behind. Pop would grimace and take deep breaths, as every bill in the mailbox was either a final notice or a termination notice.

As Christmas was swiftly approaching and Pop's job prospects were still low, he decided to earn money the best way he knew how, playing music. With me out of school three weeks for Christmas break, Pop and I would go to 34[Th] and Madison and work our way to Times Square every evening and all day on Saturdays working the streets. Pop would set his fedora on the ground upside down, and start playing music on his beloved trumpet. I was a very good dancer, and I knew all the latest moves. So, I would dance in front of him, and walkers on the street would stop and drop change in the hat. And since the streets were more packed than usual because of the holiday shopping, we could make a nice little chunk of change.

The little bit of cash Pop could scrape together helped us to survive, but it wasn't enough to handle the bills. Two days before Christmas, we came home from another afternoon of working the streets to find an eviction notice taped on the door. Pop snatched it off in disgust as he mumbled the first sentence below eviction that was typed in large letters, "In thirty days you must vacate the premises. Shit!" he yelled loudly. "In other words, get your shit and get the fuck out!"

I remember the look on my old man's face as clear as day. It's a look that no kid wants to see on their parents face. It was like he was a balloon and someone had poked him with a sharp needle. He opened the door slowly and took off his hat, "I didn't want to have to do this, but now I see I don't have a choice. Sit tight Neil; I'm going down stairs to Ms. Henry's apartment to use the phone."

Our phone was cut off a month ago, and Ms. Henry, who camps out on the front stoop daily, was nice enough to let us use her phone. Pop dropped the eviction notice on the table and took off. He returned a few hours later with this huge smile.

"C'mon over here for a minute kiddo. I got some good news," Pop said pulling out a chair for me.

"So what's happening pop?"

"I called your Uncle Socco."

"Uncle Socco?"

"C'mon Neil, you know your Uncle Socco. They use to live on the fifth floor. Your mom and I played bridge with him and Aunt Anita every Sunday after church. You used to play with his daughter who's the same age as you," Pop explained trying to jog my memory.

"Oh yeah, Uncle Socco, yeah, I remember him. They moved out west last year, right?" Uncle Socco wasn't my real uncle, but he might as well be. He and my Pop were like brothers. They were thick as thieves, and back in those days, friends that close turned into uncles.

"That's right. They moved to Texas actually. Well, Uncle Socco opened a jazz club down there, and it's doing well. He's been looking for a new band, and he said he'll give me the gig if we go down there. He even said we could stay with them until we find our own place. What do you think kiddo?"

"So...you're talking about moving to Texas?"

"I don't like it anymore than you kiddo, but we're struggling here. We're a heartbeat from being on the streets. Look, it won't be permanent. We go out there for a few months, save up a little cash, by that time your Momma will be back, and we'll move back to New York stronger than before."

I didn't like the idea at all. Matter of fact, I hated it. All my friends were here, including my girlfriend Pattie Mae. She was my first love, and when I wasn't doing homework or my chores, I was spending time with her. Every day after school, we would walk home together with me carrying her books. We'd stop at the local bodega around the corner, put our little change together, and buy jawbreakers and tootsie rolls for a penny. Shit, just last month she finally let me French kiss her for the first time in the park behind this large tree. Plus, I loved New York. I liked my school, and I didn't know any better, but I liked the Smith Projects. It was a close nit community; everyone was cool with one another. There was nothing better than a Saturday afternoon, the city would block off Madison St., and we play *stickball* and eat snow cones until the street lights came on. Our parents would look on while they pulled out card tables, smoked cigarettes, and talk major shit.

"Okay Pop," I finally muttered.

Pop walked over and put his hand on top of my head, "Don't worry kiddo. Things will work out just fine. We'll be back before you know it. You'll see."

Pop decided that the Monday after Christmas would be the day we leave. Normally, Christmas was a blissful time in the Wright house. We never really had much, but we always had each other. Every year, we had the same routine. Momma, Pop, and me would go to Rockefeller Plaza and watch the lighting of the huge Christmas tree. It was always exciting to be down there. New York was a festive place during the holidays, and the crowds were extra friendly. We'd go ice-skating while we were down there. Momma and I would laugh ourselves silly at Pop, who would fall every time his feet touched the ice. It was the only time that Pop wasn't being cool. Then we'd go home, bake and decorate sugar cookies, and sing along to old Christmas carols until the clock hit twelve. That's when we opened our gifts. It was perfect!

Now, with Momma gone, it just wasn't the same. The house felt empty, and Pop and I were emotionally drained. I spent the little free time I had saying goodbye to all my friends, while Pop was busy selling everything in the house that wasn't nailed down. On top of that, we had to work the streets even longer than normal to put together enough cash to buy train tickets to Texas.

So the first Monday after Christmas, I think it was the twenty-ninth, we left on the train for Texas. Pop had successfully sold or pawned everything we owned. The only thing we had left were the clothes on our backs, and the four small suitcases we were carrying. As we approached Grand Central Station, the feeling was bittersweet. We had been there often over the last month working the corners. The generous crowds that filled the train station over the holidays helped us to survive, but now, that station was about to help usher us out of a city I loved so dearly. I remember pressing my face against the window and staring at the Manhattan skyline until it was out of view. My breath fogged up the windows as the tears rolled down my cheeks. I could tell that even Pop was caught up in the emotion as well. He didn't think I saw it, but I caught him slyly dabbing his eyes with one of his handkerchiefs. I know we were both thinking the same thing; there is no place in the world like New York City!

The trip to Texas was long and brutal. It took three days to get there, but being black, in coach, sitting on a segregated section of the train, made three days feel like ten. The only nice thing about it was the quality time I got to spend with my old man. Since Momma left, Pop was so busy, we never really had a chance to sit down and just talk. Now, with nothing but time on our hands, Pop and I played cards and chatted the whole way. And for the first time, I thought I really had the opportunity to get to know him.

"Gin," I boasted revealing my last three cards after I pulled a seven to finish my set of sevens. I won my third consecutive game.

"Let's play something else, how about spades?" Pop asked as he threw his cards down in frustration.

"Sure," I responded smiling as I gathered up the cards and started dealing. The old man just didn't know. It didn't matter if we were playing spades or gin; pop had no chance of beating me. I was a master of any kind of card game. "So Pop, do you mind if I ask you something?"

"Of course not."

"What made you get into music? I mean what made you start playing the trumpet in the first place?"

Pop sat back in his chair, pushed the gray fedora to the back of his head, and cleared his throat. "My father, your grandpa, hip me to music when I was just a little boy. I was barely walking when he showed me how to play the piano. The man lived and breathed music. Not only was he a hell of a piano player, but he also was a great singer. There weren't too many Sundays that went by where he didn't sing lead for the church choir. That's all he ever wanted to do was sing for that little *hole in the wall* church. If he would've gotten into blues or jazz, he could've been big. Anyway, he had this huge collection of records that he played for me on this old-fashioned record player; you know the kind that you'd have to wind up. We had no television in those days, so the only thing we had to do to pass the time was listening to music. Every day, after I got out of school, he'd sit down with me in the middle of the living room floor and would play Louie Armstrong records until it was time for dinner. I fell in love with the sound of that horn from the very start. My father recognized how much I loved that sound, that on my thirteenth birthday, he bought me this trumpet," Pop said as he pulled his horn from its case, held it against his chest, and gently caressed it. "This was the best gift that my father ever gave me, that anybody ever gave me." His body was with me, but his mind went somewhere else, as he gazed up at the ceiling and started smiling.

"You never talk about grandpa or grandma, why?"

"Because the more I talk about them, the more I miss them." Grandma and grandpa was a very touchy subject with Pop. They were murdered several years ago. I never knew any details 'cause Pop would never open up and talk about it. Anytime that Momma or I would bring them up, he'd go into a shell. I guess it was his way of dealing with the pain. Like I said, my Pop was a *man's man*. He kept his emotions in check. He didn't allow his passions to run him like Momma. He turned his pain inward where Momma turned all her pain outward, especially at Pop.

"So, you knew from the start that you were going to be a musician, huh?"

"You know kiddo, sometimes things are so clear that you can't ignore them. Music is in my blood, always has been. It's who I am. The world makes sense to me when I'm playing this horn. So, I guess the answer to your question is…..yes. Playing the trumpet is my God given gift."

"So what would you do if you couldn't play anymore?"

"If I couldn't play any more…I'd die," Pop joked.

"What do you think my God given gift is, Pop?"

"I don't know kiddo. That's something you'll have to figure out on your own. I just pray that it'll be as clear to you, as it was for me."

━━◆━━

We finally arrived in Dallas around midnight on a Wednesday. Pop and I gathered our belongings and quickly excited the train. It was nice to stretch our legs and get a whiff of fresh air again after that long stuffy ride. Standing on the platform giving us orders like we were children, was this tall white man wearing these big ass boots and a faded ten-gallon hat.

As we lugged our bags full of everything we owned into the lobby of the train station, we quickly discovered that the place was completely deserted. The only people walking around were the hand full of passengers who got off at this stop. It was drastically different from Grand Central Station where there has always hundreds of people walking around anytime of the day catching trains, handing out fliers, or playing music like Pop and me. As I stood in the middle of that lobby while my eyes roamed around in astonishment, I suddenly noticed something. I had heard about them before, but never saw one in New York or even when I went to camp. It was a huge black and white sign that read, "White only water fountain." Pop and I stared at the sign for a moment, then at each other. I had never seen a sign like that before, New York had its fair share of racism, I'm sure, but not that bold and in your face. I guess living in New York shielded us from that Jim Crow way of thinking. I went to an integrated school and took a shit right alongside white boys for years. Looking around again, we quickly realized that we were the only black people in the station and everyone was staring at us like guinea pigs in a metal cage. My first thought upon taking this all in was, *I'm in hell.*

Pop began looking around for Uncle Socco but didn't see him. Gathering up our luggage, we walked outside to the front of the building to find it eerily quiet. We were in downtown Dallas and I swear; the street was so empty, that I thought tumbleweed was going to blow down Main St like one of those old spaghetti westerns. No cars driving down the street, not one cab parked on the curb. No foot traffic to speak of and the streets were dimly lit, the antithesis of New York City. I was used to seeing the Manhattan skyline lit up like a Christmas

tree every night, and multitudes of people decorating the streets all the time.

"Damn, we're early. Socco ain't expecting
us to arrive for another hour," Pop said looking
down at his watch. "You hungry?"

I nodded my head feverishly. My stomach
was growling, and I was tired of eating those
lousy salami sandwiches that pop had me fix
to last us the entire trip. Pop looked down the
street and saw a small diner with the lights on.
"C'mon, let's get a bite to eat. We got a little
time to kill."

The diner was further away then it looked.
We lumbered down two blocks carrying all our
bags until we reached the small diner. Pop had to
use his foot to push the glass door open. Just like
the train station, the diner was deserted as well,
except for these two young black guys sitting at
the other end of the counter. I was surprised to
hear a James Brown record playing on the old
jukebox, *Poppa's gotta brand new bag* I think.
Since we were in Texas, I was expecting some
Hank Williams or something. I quickly dropped
my bags and took a seat on one of the vinyl bar
stools at the counter. The aroma of food cooking
was enough to send my stomach into a frenzy.
Pop sat down beside me, and like a gentleman, he
tipped his hat to acknowledge the two guys at the
end of the bar. A black waitress wearing a pink

dress and white apron casually strolled over with her pad in hand.

"Howdy fellas, what'll it be?" she asked pulling a pencil from her hair that was pinned up.

"Can I get a cup of coffee, a soda pop for the kid, and a couple of menus," Pop replied.

"Sure thing," she responded placing two menus in front us, then reaching under the cabinet to grab a coffee cup and saucer. As she poured the coffee into the cup, she turned to me and said, "What kind soda you want? We have Coca-cola, Pepsi, RC-cola, and root beer."

"Root beer."

"What's good here?" Pop asked.

"Well, we have the meatloaf special. That comes with meatloaf, mashed potatoes, turnip greens and cornbread."

"Sounds good, we'll take two."

Sitting there waiting for the waitress to bring us our food, I couldn't help but to notice that the two guys who were sitting at the other end of the counter was staring at us. It was an uncomfortable stare. You know, creepy, especially the one on the left. He was black as tar, with a sloped forehead, big nose, and a lazy eye. Dressed in all black, he elbowed the guy next to him and got up. The lazy eye guy slowly walked over patting the pockets of his jacket and pants. Pop wasn't paying much attention to him. He was busy putting sugar and cream into his coffee trying to get it just right.

"Excuse me man, you got a light?" the strange guy asked.

"Sure," Pop answered without turning around. He was still adding more sugar to his coffee and bobbing his head to the sound of James Brown. Reaching into his pocket, he pulled out a book of matches and handed it to the guy.

"Thanks." He took his time pulling out a cigarette and lighting it. I didn't realize it then, but he was *sizing up* my old man. Sitting the book of matches down in front of Pop, he leaned over, blew out a cloud of smoke, and said, "Just got into town, huh?"

"Yeah."

"So, where you coming from?"

"New York City my man."

"Oh, okay. First time in Dallas?"

"Yeah."

"Whelp, welcome to Big D brother," he said with a grin patting Pop on the shoulder.

"Thanks," Pop replied as he turned, smiled at the guy, and shook his hand.

The guy turned toward his buddy who was still sitting at the other end of the counter and nodded his head. The other guy, a tall lanky brother with a face full of acne, got up and both guys left immediately. It was strange, but once they left; I didn't give it a second thought. By that time, the waitress had brought us our food. The grub was okay, put it couldn't touch my Momma's cooking. Still, it was better than eating those damn salami sandwiches.

With our bellies full and our belts loosen; we started on our way back to the train station. Stepping outside holding his stomach, Pop stopped, set down his bags, and began to have his customary after dinner cigarette. He looked down at his watch, took a couple of drags off his cigarette, and quickly tossed it away. "Damn, your Uncle Socco will be here any minute. We'd better get a move on," he stated grabbing his bags.

Once again, we began to lug our heavy luggage back to the train station. Making our way down the block, I vaguely heard footsteps in the distance. They sound like they were coming straight toward us, but I saw no one approaching. Pop seemed unconcern, as he was still humming the James Brown tune that was playing on the jukebox earlier. We crossed the street and were half way there, when suddenly; two shadowy figures seem to pop out of nowhere. Pop and I were startled at first, until we recognize that it was the two guys from the diner.

"Well, well, well, if it ain't New York City!" the guy with the lazy eye said sarcastically as he stood in front us with his arms behind his back, blocking our way. "You're a long way from home, brother."

"Sorry my man, we got no time. We got a ride to catch," Pop responded as he sidestepped them attempting to walk around.

"I just need your help with one little thing." Lazy eye quickly stepped over to prevent my Pop from getting away.

"What you need, man?"

"It's funny you should say that. I need everything you got," Lazy eye said as he and his partner whipped out switchblades from behind their backs. The pimple face guy snatched me up by the collar of my sweatshirt and held a knife to my throat, while Lazy eye pointed his razor-sharp blade at my Pop's nose. Pop slowly dropped his bags and raised his hands, "Easy, kid. I'll give you my wallet, just let my boy go."

"Wallet first!" Lazy eye commanded.

Pop carefully reached around to his back pocket and pulled out his wallet. He gradually held it out. Lazy eye quickly snatched it from his hand. Opening the wallet, he pulled out the little bit of cash that Pop had left and threw the wallet to the curb.

I was paralyzed with fear. I literally couldn't move. All I could think about was *I didn't want to die*. Things happened so fast, I didn't even realize that I had pissed my pants. After Lazy eye had taken the cash from my old man, the guy holding me by the shirt threw me to the ground.

"Let's get outta here!" lazy eye's partner urged as he started back peddling.

Lazy eye hesitated as he looked down at Pop's trumpet case. It looked different than the rest of the luggage we were carrying. The brand-new leather case with brass trim stood out.

"What's in the case old man?"

"Nothing but clothes," Pop lied as he picked up the case and held it close.

"Bullshit! Give it to me."

"No!"

"Give me that fucking bag old man!" Lazy eye said as he inched closer.

"You got what you came for. Now let us be."

Lazy eye reached for the case with his left hand, while the knife in his right hand was aimed at Pop's chest. Pop clutched the case tightly and backed up; he did not intend to let Lazy eye have that case. Lazy eye lunged at Pop; Pop swung the case and knocked the switchblade from his hands. There was a mad scramble for the blade as both fell to the ground. Pop's hat flew up in the air as the tussle over the blade became more intense with each punch thrown. The pimple face guy was steadily backing up and yelling, "C'mon man!" Finally, the brawl stopped, and then as if in slow motion, Lazy eye stood up with the knife in his hand, covered in blood.

"Pop!" I yelled out running over.

"C'mon Ronnie, let's get outta here!" Lazy eye's partner yelled again, as he had back peddled half way down the street by now.

Lazy eye walked over toward me, kneeled down so that we were eye to eye, pointed his blade at my face, and said, "Look here little nigga. You didn't see nothing. You dig? You tell anybody you saw me, and I'll cut your fucking eyes out." He threatens as he stumbled to his feet and ran off with his punk ass friend.

I quickly turned my attention back to my old man. Lying on the cold hard concrete, he was laboring to breathe while clutching his side.

"Pop you okay?"

"I'm alright, I'm alright. Look kiddo, you got to go get some help," he said in between gasp of breaths. "Go to the train station."

"I can't leave you Pop," I said cradling his head in my arms.

"It's okay. I'll be fine. Just go get help."

I grabbed one of the bags and used it as a pillow to prop his head up. I stood up and slowly started walking away.

"It's okay, go," he said on last time waiving me on.

I turned around and sprinted as fast as I could

back to the train station. Busting threw the doors, I saw the tall white man with the ten-gallon hat on standing by one of the counters.

"Mister, mister, I need help! My father is hurt!" I blurted out.

"Whoa, whoa, calm down boy. Now, what happened?"

"Me and my father were just mugged! They stabbed him! We need an ambulance!"

He stood there for a moment with his arms folded, sucking his teeth. "Niggas," he mumbled, "I guess I can call an ambulance." That redneck bastard took his sweet fucking time walking over to a phone before finally making the call.

I wasted no time waiting around for his country ass. I ran back to the sidewalk where my Pop was. I didn't want to leave him alone any longer than necessary. He was still lying there with his eyes closed covered in blood. I knelt down next to him, shaking him, trying to get him to wake up, but he didn't move.

"Pop, pop, wake up, wake up!" I yelled out repeatedly, but he never responded. Once again, I cradled his head in my arms, as I sat there impatiently waiting for the paramedics to show up. While trying to fight back the tears, I closed my eyes tightly, bowed my head, and started to pray, "God, please don't let my father die. Please, I'll do anything you ask. I won't talk in class. I'll eat all my vegetables. I won't stay up late, just don't let nothing happen to my Pop."

I slowly opened my eyes after I finished praying. I guess I was excepting some sort of an immediate miracle. I hoped that the strong man that my Pop was, would just spring to his feet and shake this off. That he would wipe the blood of his shirt, smile, and tell me everything is going to be okay. But it wasn't to be. Despite my pleas, God had ignored me. Pop would never open his eyes again.

January 1st 1969 my father, Raymond Neil Wright, died at the age of forty-four. It's funny how you remember those significant dates. It's now etched in my mind for as long as I live. That's because not only did my father die, but also a part of me died with him. I was hollowed out, like an old tree whose insides were rotten. I cried until I couldn't cry anymore. The police and paramedics tried on several occasions to ask me questions at the scene, but I just couldn't stop crying. For the next couple of days, I could not recall what happened at all. I don't know where I stayed or what I had eaten. All I remember was darkness and pain.

Next thing I remember was a tender touch waking me up out of my sleep. It felt like my mother's touch, soft, warm, and familiar. I immediately called for her.

"Momma," I said as I turned around and wiped my eyes.

"Hello sugar."

My eyes began to focus, and I realize that I had been sleeping on a couch in a police station. I turned around looking for my Momma. If anyone in the world knew what I was going through, it was her. I longed for her love, her soothing touch, her warm embrace to cure my aching heart. I was ready for her to tell me everything was going to be all right, and let's go home son. But I was extremely disappointed to find a strange woman smiling at me.

"My name is Mrs. Walker. I'm from social services. Your name is Neil right?" the lady asked in a tender voice while sitting down next to me and lightly grabbing my hand. She was a heavyset sister with pudgy cheeks that were painted bright red, and a pretty smile despite having gap teeth. I didn't say anything; I just nodded my head to acknowledge her.

"I'm so sorry about what happened. I can't imagine what you're going through, but I like to help, if you'll let me," Mrs. Walker commented as she leaned over and gave me hug.

"Okay," I mumbled.

"Neil, for me to help you, I'll need to ask you a few questions, sugar. Is that okay?"

"Sure."

Mrs. Walker opened a briefcase and pulled out a pen and pad to take notes. She crossed her thick legs, and gently tugged on her skirt to cover up her thighs. She was the first person that came to ask me questions that I thought was truly genuine. So, I decided to pull myself together and answer her questions.

"First of all, how do I get in touch with your family, so that I can let them know you're okay?"

"I'm not sure. My parents split up a couple of months back, and it's just been me and my pop ever since."

"So do you have a phone number for her, or an address, anything that we could use to find her?"

"She always called me. Only thing I know is that the last time I talked to her, she went back to South Carolina."

"What's her name?"

"Estelle Wright."

"Okay, I'll contact officials in South Carolina and see if they can find her. In the meantime, are there any other family members that I can contact? You know a grandparent, maybe an aunt or an uncle."

"I don't have any grandparents. They're all dead. There is my Uncle Socco. Actually, he's not my real uncle, but since him and my father are like brothers, I call him uncle. He's the reason we came to Texas in the first place. He was supposed to be meeting us at the bus station."

"You're not from Dallas?"

"No, I'm from New York. Me and my Pop

were moving out here 'cause Uncle Socco was gonna give Pop a job."

"That explains the accent," Mrs. Walker commented as she continued to jot down notes. I did have a strong New York accent. I picked it up from my Pop that had an even thicker accent from being born and raised in the Bronx.

"So what's Socco's full name?"

Scratching my head, I shrugged my shoulders and said, "I don't know. I just know him as Uncle Socco."

"Hmm…well, I'll do everything I can to find him or your mother. In the meantime, let's find you a place to stay sugar," she said putting her arm around my shoulder.

⚯

Mrs. Walker took me to some sort of transition house for the next couple of days where I got some fresh clothes and a much-needed bath. At twelve years old, taking thorough baths was not something I did with regularity. Matter of fact, I can't remember taking a bath before that day without my Momma standing over me, threatening to whip my ass with Pop's belt. But for some reason, I felt the need to bathe thoroughly. It was like my soul was dirty as well as my skin. I'd been wearing the same blood-drenched clothes since the attack. Pop's blood had dried up not only on my skin, but on my pants and shirt too. I peeled off those dirty rags and scrubbed and scrubbed thinking that, somehow, someway; I could cleanse myself of this whole ordeal. But it was no use. I'd been changed forever.

That next morning my Pop was laid to rest at this place called Potter's Field. It was a shitty cemetery just on the outskirts of downtown Dallas where they buried the poor, homeless, or Jon Doe's that nobody claimed. There were no headstones in front of any of the graves, only a wooded stake with the name of the dead carved into it. The place was poorly kept. The grass was uncut. Some of the stakes had blown over, and trash had blown up against the metal fence that surrounded the cemetery.

It was freezing cold that morning. The wind was howling and there was an overcast that completely blocked out the sun. I stood next to Mrs. Walker, who had her arm around my shoulder trying to show as much compassion as one can to a stranger. There were only five people there that morning, me, Mrs. Walker, the officer who was handling the case, the police department Chaplin, and the ground's keeper. The Chaplin said a few generic words that I couldn't remember, or maybe I just don't want to, and then I walked over and took one last peek into the coffin. Unknowingly, they buried Pop in his favorite black suit, which was the only thing right about the whole funeral. The moment I stepped back, the ground's keeper put the lid on a cheap ass wooden box they put Pop in, and started nailing it shut. Every time he reared back and struck a nail with his hammer. My heart would flutter. It was surreal. I watched with my own eyes and still couldn't believe this was actually happening. I felt so helpless. My father was dead and there wasn't shit I could do about it!

I walked over, placed my hands on the coffin, and closed my eyes. "I'll be back for you, Pop. I won't leave you in this place. I promise." I vowed as the tears came streaming down my face. For me, it wasn't goodbye. It was see you later.

My life was in shambles. It felt like one of those thousand piece jigsaw puzzles that takes months to put to together, and someone just comes along and messes it all up. Now I have to put the pieces back together again. There's only one problem, I'm twelve-years old and I don't have a clue how.

The next two weeks went by at an insufferable slow pace. I sat around the living room at the transition house in a daze, twiddling my thumbs waiting to hear some word from my momma. Occasionally, I watched a little TV when one of my favorite shows was on, like Get Smart. But even the funniest comedies couldn't take my mind off the pain I was feeling.

I woke up early that Monday morning feeling optimistic for the first time in weeks. Mrs. Walker, who'd placed me in that transition house in the first place, said she was coming by today. *They finally got in touch with my momma, and she's finally coming to get me,* I thought. I washed up and got dressed in the best outfit I had, a white button-down shirt, khaki pants, and some brown penny-loafers momma had bought me last Easter. I sat on the couch staring at the front door eagerly awaiting her arrival by eight o'clock in the morning.

Mrs. Walker finally wandered through the front door a couple of hours later. Lugging her large briefcase and dressed professional as normal, Mrs. Walker walked over toward me with her face wearing a somber look. I paid no attention to her as I hopped off the couch and sprinted to the front door looking for my momma.

"Hello Mrs. Walker," I said.

"Hello sugar," Mrs. Walker said with a forced grin flashing those gap teeth of hers.

"Where's my momma at? I don't see her anywhere," I asked peaking through the curtains.

"Come have a seat sugar," she suggested patting the seat next to her on the couch. I reluctantly came over and sat down next to her. She placed one of her meaty hands on my knee and leaned in closer. "Neil, I don't how to tell you this, but.... we haven't been able to locate your mother or this Socco fellow you told me about."

I sunk back in my seat, completely deflated and beaten.

"Don't worry sugar; we're going to keep on looking for your mother. In the meantime, I'm going to have to take you to another place."

"What's wrong with the place," I replied looking around the room.

"This is a temporary place. They're not equipped to take care of you long term."

"What do you mean long term? My mom is coming to get me, ain't she?" I asked with pleading eyes.

"Of course she is sugar. It just might take a little longer than we first thought. Now, why don't you gather up all of your things?"

"Where are we going?"

"I'm taking you to The Holmes School for Boys."

———

I packed up all my things, plus my pop's stuff, including his trumpet, and hopped in Mrs. Walker's broken-down jalopy. The car ride was an adventure in itself, because she couldn't drive a lick. I spent the majority of the twenty-minute trip with my eyes closed clinching the dashboard of her beat-up Buick Roadmaster while she bobbed and weaved out of traffic nearly hitting every car in sight. Thank God, she had good breaks.

As we drove outside the city and into this small country town of Seagoville, the street ended and the gravel-paved road began. Soon, the only thing I saw in every direction was trees and large fields of hay with cattle grazing on it. We turned into this long winding driveway that led up this huge cathedral looking building that was so old and decrepit, that a good stiff breeze could knock it over. Uneasiness came over me as we approached, not even the soulful sound of *The Chilites* playing on Mrs. Walker's radio could calm my nerves. I guess the first sign that this place was trouble was the fact that a barbwire fence surrounded the place. In my experiences, fences are only design to do one of two things, keep people out, or keep people in. And the last time I checked, nobody was trying to break into an orphanage.

Walking through the massive foyer, we were quickly greeted by an overly friendly man with a stack of papers under his arm, "Hello Mrs. Walker," he said grinning ear to ear. This wiry white man with round spectacles and hair protruding from every place on his head, including his ears, shook her hand so long and furiously that she literally had to snatch it back. "So, is this the little fellow you were telling me about?" he asked her rubbing me on top of the head and messing up my natural. I can't tell you how irritating that was. Nothing made more furious as a kid then someone rubbing my head.

"Yes Mr. Goodwin. This handsome young man's name is Neil," Mrs. Walker responded.

"Good, why don't you two step into my office," he said as he walked across the hallway and open the door for us. "Please, have a seat."

We sat my bags down in the hallway and followed him into his musty office that smelled like a combination of sweaty feet and rat poison. The odor seemed to originate from a set of sweats and old running shoes that he cleared of the seats so that we could sit down. "Sorry about that. I wasn't expecting ya'll so soon. I had to get my morning workout in." He joked, as he casually tossed the clothes into a small cabinet, plopped down in his chair, and kicked his feet up on his wooden desk.

"Here is all the paperwork dealing with his case," Mrs. Walker stated reaching into her briefcase and handing over my file. "Now, Neil is special. I told him that you would take good care of him here until I can find his family."

"Of course we'll take good care of him. There's nothing to worry about, he's in good hands," he said flashing this cheesy grin.

"Good. Well, Neil," she said turning toward me. "This is goodbye for now. But like I said, don't worry. I'm gonna be checking up on you often, and I'll continue the search for your family in the meantime, okay."

"Okay," I answered trying to perk up a little.

Mrs. Walker grabbed her suitcase, gave me

a tremendous hug, and head down the hallway. I stood there with my shoulder's slumped counting the steps until she left out the door.

"Hey," Mr. Goodwin blurted out snapping me out of my trance. The sudden harsh sound of his voice made me straighten up and turn around immediately. This delightfully easygoing man's demeanor quickly changed. His pale face went through a complete metamorphous. It was as if someone waived a magic-wand in his face and caused that cheesy looking grin to change into an ugly smirk.

"Yes sir."

"Take a seat and listen up kid, 'cause I'm only gonna say this once," he ordered pushing the long stringy hair out of his face and hooking it behind his ears. He reached into the top drawer of his desk, pulled out a small manual, and tossed it into my lap. "These are the rules of this building. Read it! Know it! Everything is in this facility, including your school, and dormitory where you'll live. Breakfast is at seven, school starts at eight o'clock sharp. You're not allowed to leave the premises under any circumstances. Violation of any rules will result in loss of privileges. You will be assigned to dorm six. Any problems, you take them to your Dorm Director first. Understand?"

"Yes sir," I replied trying to soak up the sudden burst of information.

"Excellent!" Mr. Goodwin said as he hit the intercom button, "Mark, get down here!" he yelled. "Mark is your Dorm Director. He'll show you where you're staying and where to put your things."

I walked into the hallway with Mr. Goodwin following closely behind. While grabbing my suitcase of clothes and the case that held pop's trumpet, I could hear the footsteps of someone approaching from around the long corridor. An extremely tall guy, who was black as midnight, wearing a pair of gym shorts and a wife-beater t-shirt strolled up whistling some funny tune. He stopped right in front of me, folded his muscular arms, looked down at me with this crooked smile, and said, "Damn, another new fish?"

"That's right. And watch your language!" Mr. Goodwin interjected stepping between us. "Mark this is Neil, Neil this is Mark. Mark, take Neil to the dorm and show him his bunk."

"Sure thing," Mark answered as he rolled his eyes at Mr. Goodwin on the sly. "C'mon man," he said gesturing for me to follow him. He abruptly turned around and started briskly walking down the hall without offering to help me carry any of my bags. I struggled to keep up with him with toting all my things. As I got closer to him, I could smell this funky scent that seemed to follow him around like the cloud of dirt that followed Pig-Pen from *Charlie Brown*.

"So where you from fish?" Mark asked.

"Huh?" I said trying to understand what he was saying. He had this thick country accent that was so difficult to make out.

"Where you from? What, you don't speak English or something nigga?"

After I finally realized what he was asking, I mumbled, "New York."

"Shit, you a long way from home," he replied, and then he slowed down until we were side by side. He took a long hard stare at me, looking me up and down several times as we approached the dormitory. Leaning closer, he put his arm around my shoulder, licked his lips and whispered, "Don't worry about anything my man. I run this place. As long as you do what I say, when I say, you'll be just fine."

We walked in the room to find the other kids huddled around a small black-and-white television watching Speed Racer. The room was a disaster zone. It looked like a grenade had gone off in the center scattering clothes everywhere. The wooden floor was littered with filthy socks and underwear with nasty shit stains. Mark led me past the boys and through the debris to a small, metal, twin bed with a large footlocker at the end that resembled something from an army boot camp.

"Here is your bunk," Mark said standing at

the foot of the bed with his hands on his hips, "By the way, new fish get bathroom duty. So make sure you handle that after supper."

I nodded my head and proceeded to settle in. I felt like a guinea pig in a cage unpacking my clothes as I could feel the cold stares from the other boys. I finally finished putting my things away as the other kids turned their attention back to the cartoons. Sitting on the edge of my bed, I nervously twiddled my thumbs. Then a loud bell rang. The boys scrambled to their feet and quickly shuffled out the door.

One kid lagged behind. A chubby light skinned boy with freckles. He waited until the other boys left and waddled over toward me. "Don't mind them. They hate new fish. They call me Frito. What's your name?" he said offering his hand.

"Neil," I replied shaking his hand firmly. I started to ask why they called him Frito, until I noticed the small bag of Frito Lay corn chips sticking out of the side of his pocket.

"Solid," he replied.

"What's a fish?" I asked.

"New guy, you know, fresh on the scene like a fish," he joked, "You sure talk funny, where you from?"

"New York."

"Wow, you're from New York. That's so cool. I always wanted to go there."

"For real?"

"Hell yeah, New York is bad ass. Plus, my team plays there."

"Who?"

"Joe Namath and the Jets!" Frito said with a huge smile.

"That was my Pop's favorite team. He used to take me to the games all the time."

"Damn, you and your Pop hangout like that. I can dig-it man. Shit, I never even met my old man. He could walk through that door right now and I wouldn't even know what he looks like," he commented with his eyes closed and his head hanging low, "If you don't mind me asking, what are you doing here?"

Frito was so easy going, that I had no reluctance spilling my guts. "Well, my parents split up last year. So my Pop decided to move down here for a while to play in a band at my Uncle's nightclub. But on our way here, we got mugged and the guys killed him. Mrs. Walker said I have to stay here for a little bit while they find where my momma is. Soon as she finds out I'm here, she'll come get me."

"She told me the same thing. That one of my family members would come pick me up any day. That was four years ago. Face it bro, you're stuck here like the rest of us."

His words were sobering. It never once

crossed my mind that my momma wouldn't come get me. I always thought she was probably somewhere in South Carolina worried sick about me and Pop. But his words planted the seed of doubt in my head for the first time. *It's been almost three weeks, why hasn't she came by now*, I thought. Then the bell rang for the second time breaking me out of my trance. Frito sprung to his feet, "I almost forgot, that was the dinner bell. Let's split before all the grub is gone."

I followed behind Frito as he led the way into the cafeteria. The brick walls that were painted with a bland white and the long wooden tables made the place feel more like a prison cafeteria. It was extremely noisy as the chatter and silverware clinging against plastic trays filled the air. The ladies behind the counter shot us dirty looks for being late. They dumped a nice helping of pinto beans, rice, and a slice of cornbread. No meat at all, damn! The rest of the boys from all three dorms, about forty kids in all, had already had their trays and were throwing down. We took a seat by ourselves at the far end of the table that the rest of the guys from our dorm were seated at. After taking a couple of bites, I immediately wanted to spit that nasty shit out, but I was so hungry that I ate it anyway.

"So is anybody else around here cool like you?" I asked.

"Ain't nobody cool like me," Frito joked in between bites, "But most of these guys are alright. It just takes them a while to warm up to a new fish. You got to watch out for some people in here. Everybody can't be trusted."

"What about Mark? He seems cool."

"Sodom! You don't wanna mess with him. That nigga is bad news," Frito whispered while leaning closer. His lighthearted demeanor swiftly changed.

"Why do you call him Sodom?"

"I hope you never have to find out," he warned as he cut his hazel eyes at Mark, who was sitting at the other end of the table. "Just stick with me, I'll show you the ropes."

"So should I clean the bathroom like he said?"

"Yeah, ain't no way around that. Every new fish gets bathroom duty. Don't worry though, we get new fish in all the time, and the next guy will take your place."

So after dinner, Frito took me to the supply closet and showed me what I needed to clean the bathroom. I had never cleaned a bathroom at that point. Since my momma was a housewife, she did all the cooking and cleaning. Only thing I was responsible for was cleaning my room. After grabbing a mop, rags, ammonia, and bottle of bleach, I followed Frito to the large bathroom that was next to our dorm.

"Good luck," Frito said with a frowned face pushing the door open with one hand, and pinching his nose closed with the other.

I walked in, and I swear; the smell of piss was so fucking strong; I literally thought I burnt off my nostrils. I immediately dropped everything, covered my face, and coughed uncontrollably. Propping the door open with the mop bucket, it took a minute before the air circulated enough where I could tolerate the smell. Every single toilette seat was saturated with piss and pubic hair. The showers were filthy. I didn't really know how to clean, and judging from my predecessor; he didn't either, but I knew bleach smelled better than piss, so I poured it on everything in sight.

After scrubbing that bathroom until my knees were sore, I was ready to crash. I put away the cleaning supplies and made it back to the dorm just in time for the evening count and mandatory lights out. Mr. Goodwin strolled through the door without saying a word. Everybody snapped to attention and stood in front of their beds like Mr. Goodwin was a drill sergeant. He quickly counted heads then hit the lights as he left the room.

Physically and mentally exhausted, I climbed into my rock-hard bed. Most of the guys are in their bunks softly whispering back and forth to each other. The dimly lit hallway kept our dorm from being pitch-black. As tired as I was, I couldn't fall asleep. I just didn't feel comfortable enough. I found myself staring at the oversize rat climbing into my shoe using it as a bed. I turned around, put my hands together, and started to pray, "God, I know I don't pray as much as I should, but I really need you now. Please send my Momma to come get me. I miss her so much. And please keep me safe in here and watch over me. In Jesus' name, Amen."

I suffered through a long sleepless night. By the time the bells ranged for breakfast that next morning, I was already dressed, sitting on the edge of my bed, twirling my thumbs. The other kids slowly started moving around. They looked at me rather oddly, but continued not to speak. I noticed something strange as everyone peeled off the covers and began climbing out of bed. They were all fully dressed, even Frito.

"So, how was your first night?" Frito asked, as he casually strolled over and took a seat on my bed next to me.

"Rough."

"Nothing happened, did it," he whispered leaning closer.

"Like what," I replied confused.

"Never mind."

Then I smelled a funky scent and I felt a hand firmly touching my shoulder. Frito felt the same touch, as we both turned around in unison to find Mark gazing at us with a devilish grin. "What you boys over here whispering about?"

"Nothing," Frito murmured turning his head

away in disgust. It was obvious that Mark's touch irritated him.

"New York City, my man," Mark said turning toward me, "You know there're a lot of things I always wanted to know about New York."

"Like what?" I asked.

"Like how good the pussy is."

I stared at him batting my eyes with a blank expression. As absurd as it might sound now, I had never heard the word *pussy* before. I was a sheltered child. It's not like it is now, where every little foul mouth punk roaming the streets casually tosses it around like an adjective to describe everything.

"What's a matter boy, you hard of hearing or something?" Mark added.

"No," I responded shrugging my shoulders.

"Maybe later tonight, we can get better acquainted," Mark suggested looking me up and down again. He turned his attention back to Frito and slapped him on the shoulder, "Ain't that right Fats."

Frito didn't utter a word. He just rolled his eyes. Springing to his feet, he turned toward me said, "C'mon Neil, let's get some grub."

―――

After a terrible Saturday morning breakfast, everybody congregated in the large courtyard outside. It was equipped with swings, sand traps, and monkey bars for the small kids, and for the older ones, there was a basketball court, a handball court and a small football field. The morning overcast and freezing air discouraged no one from going outside. Saturday and Sunday was the only time that Mr. Goodwin and the administration allowed us outside.

As Frito and I stepped outside, we saw the other guys from our dorm huddled up in a small circle, shivering their asses off. One of them poked his head out and motioned toward Frito to come over.

"Hang loose, I'll be right back," Frito ordered as he strolled over and disappeared inside the huddle. I heard a bunch of gabbing, but nothing I could make out. After a few minutes, they broke the huddle like a team of football players and started walking toward me with serious looking faces. The leader of the pack, a midget looking nigga stepped out front. "What's up blood, they call me Mousey," he stated in a high-pitched voice sounding like Tattoo from *Fantasy Island*. It was easy to understand how he got that nickname. Facing me, his ears looked like a car with the doors wide open. His nose was long and thin and he had this pitiful looking mustache that resembled a cat's whiskers. "We hear your name is Neil and you're from New York?"

"Yeah, that's right."

"So Frito tells us you wanna hang with us?"

I turned and looked at Frito, who winked his eye at me. So I nodded at dude.

"To hang with us, you got to go through an initiation."

"What I gotta do?" I eagerly inquired.

Mousey reached behind his back and pulled out a white paper cup. He locked his beady eyes with mine and slowly extended the cup for me to take, "Everyone has to take a sip from *the cup of purity* to hang with us."

I took the cup from his stubby little hands and stared at it rather oddly for a long time. The liquid was a gold colored and smelled weird. "What is it?"

"It's beer," he answered, as he turned and smiled at the other guys.

I looked at it closely one more time with a frowned up face, "All you guys drunk this?"

"That's right!" they all responded in unison, nodding their heads in agreement.

"Okay," I said gradually lifting the cup toward my mouth; the other guys moved closer and looked on with great anticipation. Their eyes widened as I took a sip. As soon as the taste of that shit hit my tongue, I spit it out and yelled, "Fuck!" at the top of my lungs. It was the first time I cursed since my momma washed my mouth out with a bar of soap when she caught me saying *damn* in front of the stoop. "This ain't beer!"

All the guys, including Frito, were on the ground holding their stomachs, rolling in laughter. "We know," Mousey joked.

I put the cup close to my nose one more time, and really took a good sniff, "Piss, ugh!" I yelled, throwing the cup in their direction and gagging uncontrollably trying to force myself to cough up every disgusting drop of that nasty shit. I licked my shirt trying to get the taste off my tongue.

Frito was in tears he was laughing so hard, and Frito had one of those infectious laughs. You know the type; that's so jolly and goofy that when you hear it, you just got to laugh yourself no matter how you feel. Therefore, after watching him cracking up, rolling around on the ground like a hog in slop, I caught myself giggling a little bit too.

Mousey finally managed to climb back to his feet and stopped laughing long enough to say, "No matter how many times we do that shit, it still makes me laugh." Covering his mouth with his hand to keep from laughing in my face, he walked over to me and gave me some skin, "Don't sweat that shit blood; we've all taken that drink before."

"It's cool," I said with an uncomfortable grin.

"You a good sport, I like that. I now proclaim you an official member of D6."

"D6?" I asked.

"Dorm 6 baby," Mousey responded, "C'mon, I'll introduce you around. This skinny, ugly looking ass nigga here is Gil."

"Fuck you Mousey!" Gil yelled out with his middle finger up.

Mousey just chuckled and casually waved him off and pointed to the next guy, "The white boy with the long stringy hair is Jake. The big-headed nigga over there is Mitch, and you already know Frito."

Each one of them walked over and happily gave me some skin. I think that was the first time since I arrived where I truly felt comfortable and accepted. I didn't want to be there, but if had to, it was nice to have a few friends.

⟨⟨⟨⟩⟩⟩

After a long day of basketball, marbles, and freeze tag, we prepared for the evening count. Mr. Goodwin casually strolled in at his usual time. I don't think he actually looked at us when he did his bed check. I think to him, we were just bodies. As long as he could account for us physically, I don't think he really cared.

I settled into my bunk dressed in a wife-beater and boxers. That's how I felt comfortable sleeping. I easily sweat for some reason. I noticed that everyone else was bundled up tight. Shit, Frito climbed into bed fully clothed in dungarees and a sweatshirt. It was very peculiar since Mr. Goodwin had the heat turned up. Kind of odd, but I didn't give it a second thought.

The lights went out and I rolled over on my stomach and punched my rigid pillow several times, as I tried to get comfortable. The room was incredibly dark again except for those hall lights. The faint sound of bare feet walking across the wooden floor woke me out of my light slumber. I paid it no mind as I finally started to doze off after a few minutes. Then I could feel the springs in my bed squeaking, and before I could move, I felt pressure on top of me pinning me down. My eyes popped open as I tried to swing my head around to see what's going on, but a large firm hand pushed my head back down on my pillow. I couldn't turn around, but I smelled that familiar funky scent. It was Mark, and his sweaty, naked body was pressed up against me.

"Don't move," Mark ordered with his voice barely above a whisper as he pushed a sharp knife against my throat just enough to barely break the skin.

"Please don't hurt me. I didn't do anything?" I said although Mark's body weight was crushing my chest, and I was struggling to breathe.

"Shhh," he murmured putting the knife up to his lips as if it were his index finger. He leaned forward and pressed his lips against my ear, "You know normally I like to wait awhile and let the anticipation build. It's like foreplay to me. But when I saw you, hmmm, I couldn't resist." I cut my eyes just enough to see Mark lick his crust lips.

"Man, I don't know what you're talking about. What do you want?"

"I want to taste that New York pussy," he replied sliding his other hand under the sheets. I felt him sticking one of his long fingers inside me. The strange sensation caused my body to seize up. I tried to get away, but Mark's body weight on top of me was too heavy for me to wiggle away.

"No, stop!" I tried to yell, but it sounded more like a whisper because my lungs were still restricted. I looked around to see if anyone else was up and could help. As my eyes quickly scan the dark room, I could see the white in those kids' eyes. When they saw me look at them, they all turned around and pulled the sheets over their heads. No one lifted a finger to help, not even Frito.

"Don't fight it New York, it'll make things go faster."

"Please, stop!" I begged.

"Shut the fuck up New York!" Mark ordered

shoving the knife against my throat once again, "Before I get blood on my knife, instead of shit on my dick."

Mark took his knife and sliced open the back of my boxer shorts. Placing his other hand over my mouth, he began to insert himself inside of me. It was incredibly painful as I squirmed, wiggled, and clinched my butt cheeks trying to fend him off, but Mark was determined. He forced himself in me and started stroking with reckless abandon. I felt like my insides were being ripped to shreds. I grinded my teeth, closed my eyes tightly, and bared the pain as best I could. It may have been just a few minutes in reality, but it felt like an eternity to me. Watching my momma leave stripped me of my youth, watching my father die stripped me of my innocence, being sent to an orphanage stripped me of my dignity, but Mark raping me…stripped me of everything I had left.

The bell for breakfast that next morning seemed louder than normal. I wasn't sleep, but the sound was still jarring. I was tired and my eyelids were heavy as hell, but I didn't get a wink of sleep. My asshole was throbbing something terrible, and blood had trickled down my thighs as if I were a woman on her cycle. When the lights popped on, I pulled the covers over my head and curled up in ball hoping that no one would notice. I felt so ashamed, so weak, and so helpless. Plus, I didn't want the other kids to see that I'd been crying all night long. I could faintly hear the boys scurrying about, getting ready for breakfast. They were quieter than normal, not all the hoopla that usually accompanied their morning ritual. After I heard the last footsteps leave the room, I exhaled in relief, and then I felt a tap on my shoulder that sent a shockwave through my body causing me to recoil in fear.

"It's me, Frito," he said taking a seat on the edge of my bed.

I looked at him for a moment in disgust and

then pulled the sheets back over my head. "Leave me alone," I murmured.

"You alright man?"

"Just leave me alone Frito."

"Look, I know what you're going through. Here, take this."

I pulled back the sheets and poked my head out to see that Frito was holding a washcloth.

"After you take a shower, stick this iced cold rag that I snuck out of the kitchen in you. It'll help with the pain. The bleeding will stop in a day or two."

I was furious with Frito, but I took the rag, nonetheless. I rolled out of the bed and stood on my feet gingerly. The pain was excruciating as I walked bowlegged into the bathroom. Throwing away my bloody, cut up boxers, I washed up and did just as Frito suggested. I took a deep breath and wedged that cold rag in between my butt cheeks as if were a tampon. And you know what, Frito was right, it did feel a little bit better.

I went back to my bunk and pulled out my Pop's trumpet case. Guess I just wanted something to remind me of home. I took out his horn and sat there admiring it for a moment. It was still shining from the last time he polished it. I held it close to my chest as thoughts of Pop teaching me the scales in our old apartment resonated in my head. Sticking out the side of one of the pockets, I noticed an old picture. Pulling it out to get a closer look, I saw that it was Pop and I at my third birthday party. We had the biggest smiles on our faces as I was on my Pop's shoulders with my face smeared with cake and ice cream. The site of that picture crushed the little bit of spirit that I had left. I looked to see if the coast was clear, then I fell to my knees with tears in my eyes and began to pray, "God, please send my momma for me, and protect and keep me safe until she can get me. Please God."

I stayed in my bunk all day skipping breakfast, lunch, but by dinner, I was hungry. So I went down to the cafeteria to get some grub. On tonight's menu was chicken dumplings and cornbread. I grabbed my tray and sat at the far end of an empty table trying to ignore the stares from the other guys in my dorm. With my head down eating my food, I could sense someone approaching. I looked up and saw Frito holding his tray. "You mind if I sit down?" he asked.

"If you want."

"So, how you feeling man?"

"How you think I'm feeling?"

"I guess that was dumb question. Look, I know what you're going through. Sodom has gotten all of us. I was going to warn you. I just didn't think he was going to make his move so fast," Frito revealed taking a bit of food.

"Why don't somebody do something?"

"Do what? He's the baddest, toughest, nigga in here."

"What about going to Mr. Goodwin? He can do something about it, can't he?"

"You think you got problems now; get labeled a snitch in here. Let me tell you something, the only thing worse than a nigga like Sodom is a snitch. So ain't nobody telling Goodwin shit, and if you know what's good for you, don't you think about telling Goodwin shit either," Frito said shaking his head, "Look at it this way Neil, he'll be eighteen in ten months."

"So!"

"So, when you turn eighteen they release you. We just got to wait him out bro. Don't worry. Ten months will go by before you know it."

⸺◦⸺

Not only did time not fly by. It came to a grinding halt. The routine torture of being victimized was nothing I could get used to. We all suffered, Mousey, Frito, Gill, even white boy Jake, but none suffered as much as me. I was his favorite for some reason, and nothing I did deterred Mark's advances. Going to bed fully dressed or sleeping on my back was unless. No matter what I did, he visited my bunk more than the others. Only thing I did was continue to pray every day hoping that God would eventually answer it.

Things continued on that way until March. Just like normal kids, we get a week out of school for spring break, but Mr. Goodwin gave us no rest. He marched into our dorm early Monday morning just after the lights popped on.

"Rise and shine boys," he stated clapping his hands loudly.

The boys all let out a collective groan, so did I. We all thought that if we didn't get to do anything else during our spring break that we would at least be able to sleep in.

Mr. Goodwin took off his round spectacles and wiped them clean. Pushing his long hair out of the way, he clapped his hands again and raised his voice even louder, "Let's go, on your feet," Mr. Goodwin ordered like he was some drill sergeant and we were some recruits. "Just because ya'll got a couple of days off, doesn't mean ya'll be in here loafing. We have guest next week, so it's time for some spring-cleaning. I want this place thoroughly cleaned from top to bottom, and all your belongings neatly stowed away in your footlockers. Mark will be assigning ya'll specific task. So let's get cracking!"

Mr. Goodwin abruptly left the room and proceeded to the next dorm, as Mark came strutting up in just his draws scratching his nuts, with his chest poked out. "Alright ya'll little niggas, listen up! Frito, you sweep and mop the floors. Mousey, you clean the windows. Gil, you and Mitch clean the walls, and Neil you clean the bathroom."

"Shit!" I said under my breath. I was hoping I'd get a break. I hated always having to clean that nasty, piss infested bathroom.

I grabbed the cleaning supplies, but before I could get started, Mr. Goodwin popped his head back in the door, "Neil, can I see you in my office."

I walked down to his office to see Mrs. Walker standing by his front door sharply dressed holding her briefcase. I was instantly elated. *She found my Momma and she's here to take me home* I thought. I was so overcome with joy that I actually smiled for the first time in months.

"Hello Neil," Mrs. Walker said.

"Hi. So, where's my mom?" I asked looking around grinning from ear to ear, "She out in the car or something? Do I need to go pack up my things?" I was anxious, bubbling with energy, ready to go.

"Ugh, not exactly," she replied scratching her head, "Neil, I think you better have a seat."

"What do I need to sit down for? You gonna take me to my momma right?"

She sat down next to me and tried to put her arm around my shoulder. Her touch made me flashback to the first time that Mark violated me. It was like I was reliving that horrific moment all over again. I quickly twisted and contorted my body to keep Mrs. Walker from touching me. It didn't matter that she was a woman. I didn't like for anyone to touch my body at all anymore.

"You alright?" she asked.

I looked over and saw Mr. Goodwin staring at me. I wanted to tell Mrs. Walker everything I had been through, but I was scared to say anything with Mr. Goodwin around. Without saying a word, Mr. Goodwin's eyes said *don't air our dirty laundry.* So I just lowered my head and mumbled, "I'm fine, I just wanna see my momma."

"Well that's going to be a problem. We weren't able to find your mother Neil."

"I don't understand. How could you not find her? I told you where she's at."

"I'm sorry. We did everything we could, but there's no sign of her."

"So what happens now?"

"You'll have to stay here."

I didn't hear anything else after she said that. She might as well have been a mime; because there wasn't shit she was talking about that I was interested in hearing. The thought of being in this hellhole another day hurt me to my soul. I got up and walked out without saying another.

The walk down the hallway, back to the dorm, was the longest I ever took. With everything that transpired over the last few months, I never doubted, not even for one moment, that momma would come get me, until now. Dejected, I walked into the dorm and couldn't believe my eyes. Mark was on my bed carelessly twirling around my Pop's trumpet.

"Where you been New York, you got work to do?" Mark asked.

"That's my father's trumpet, put it down!" I snapped ignoring his question.

"What this?" he joked tossing it up in the air and then catching it behind his back.

"Stop it before you break it!" I said, as I charged him trying to take it back. He held the horn high up in the air with his long arm while taunting me. I hopped on the bed trying to get closer, but he pushed me off him with the greatest of ease.

"This is my horn now!" Mark joked.

"C'mon Mark, stall him out!" Frito interjected walking over trying to help me.

"Shut up Fats and get back to work!" Mark ordered pushing him in the face as Frito fell to the floor.

Mousey quit washing the windows. He slowly made his way over with his arms folded and his beady eyes locked on Mark. Even Gil and Mitch came walking out of the bathroom holding the mop and broom.

"What you niggas looking at? Get ya'll ass back to work!" Mark shouted, but nobody moved. We all stood there as if our feet were in concrete. I was stunned by the reaction, so was Mark. He had this confused look as his eyes darted back and forth between us. He towered over the rest of us, but it was five of us, and only one of him.

"Fine," Mark said sarcastically, "Here's your little horn." He casually flipped it over toward me. I quickly reached for it, but it didn't come over far enough, and it hit the floor and bounced under the bed.

"Oops," Mark joked, as he smirked walking out the front door.

Reaching under the bed, I grabbed the horn to find it bent in a couple of different places. My blood was boiling. Fucking with me was one thing, fucking with my old man's horn was another. Sitting on the edge of my bed staring at my Pop's trumpet for a moment, I had what drug addicts call a *moment of clarity*. My Momma is not coming for me. God is not going to answer my prayers. Mr. Goodwin does give a shit. I have no other family to depend on. I'm on my own! That's when the switch was flipped on inside of me. I'm not taking shit from Mark or anyone else again.

Later that evening after dinner, I went to the bathroom to wash up for bed. My mind was still preoccupied with what happen earlier, so I was really in a trance as I brushed my teeth and washed my face. Normally, we try to stay together when using the bathroom at night so that Mark wouldn't catch us alone, but I was so *out of it* that when I wiped my face off, I realized I was by myself. I got fully dressed in a t-shirt and dungarees and gathered my things together when I heard the door squeak open.

"Hi," Mark said. He snuck in and so did that familiar funky smell of his. "What's wrong, you not happy to see me?" he asked with a sneaky looking grin.

I didn't say anything, I just dropped my things and stood there staring at him. My mind was functioning different for the first time. Before I would've been crying pleading with him not to hurt me, but now, I was thinking how I could get even. I rubbed the side of my pants and re-membered I still had a box cutter from when I was breaking down boxes earlier when we were spring-cleaning.

"You don't seem so brave without your friends around New York," he said slowly approaching, "I think you've been spending too much time with them, getting a smart mouth. I think I need to do something with that smart mouth of yours."

"Like what?" I replied calmly.

He looked down at the front of his pants and began pulling down his zipper. "You're going to get on your knees and make it better." Reaching into his draws, he whipped out his Johnson and dangled it in front of me.

"Okay," I said falling to my knees. I grabbed it with my right hand and stroked it a couple of times until he was fully aroused and at ease. Tilting his head back, he exhaled and his eyes rolled into the back of his head. I carefully reached into my pocket and pulled out the box cutter. Pushing out the razor blade, I waited until Mark was fully erect. At his most vulnerable, with his eyes closed tightly and moaning with pleasure, I took a hard fast swipe and sliced his dick at the base. The blade was slightly dull, so it didn't quite cut it all the way off. Some of the skin and muscle still kept it connected as it dangled from his body pouring out blood. Mark's scream was so loud, long, and high pitched that it sounded like one those sirens that alert you when there's a storm.

"You don't seem so tough without your dick," I said dropping the blade on him. The boys rushed in to see Mark rolling around on the floor, holding his Johnson, and screaming like a little girl. I washed my hands, walked over to my bunk, and laid down and got me some rest.

———◦◦◦———

After the commotion was over, and the ambulance left, Mr. Goodwin had us lined up in his office. I could literally see steam rising off the top of his head as he paced back and forth. This went on for a few minutes. He didn't say anything; he just paced back and forth occasionally shooting us this dirty look. Running his fingers through his long hair, Mr. Goodwin finally stopped and turned toward us with hands on his hips. "What the hell just happen!" he eventually blurted out.

Nobody said anything; we all stood there staring back at him like our mouths were glued shut.

"Hello," Mr. Goodwin yelled snapping his fingers and making wild gestures, "Am I talking to myself? What the hell just happen?"

The guys continued to stay mute. Mr. Goodwin was beside himself with anger. "You think this is a game? What, you think it's funny to cut off a boy's dick? I want to know who's responsible right now!" he demanded.

Despite the ranting and raving, the boys continued to stay quiet. Frito wasn't bullshitting; the no snitching code he told me about was true, these boys weren't going to say one single word. I couldn't resist though. I stepped forward, locked eyes with him, and said, "Mr. Goodwin, maybe if you took your head out of your ass and paid a little attention, you'd know what was going on."

Mousey and Frito leaned forward with their jaws on the floor staring at me from the side in astonishment. Mr. Goodwin, who wore a similar look, slowly turned his back toward us and put his hands on his hips. "Get out my office," he mumbled.

We marched out of his office single file back to the dorm. I sat down on the edge of my bunk gazing up at the ceiling as the thoughts of everything that just happened swirled around in my head. Then Frito walked up to me with the other boys following closely behind. He grabbed my hand and gave me some dap, "Thank you bro. I owe you." Mousey was next, he expressed the same sentiments. So did Gil, Mitch, and white boy Jake. I must admit. I loved the show of admiration and respect from them. It was intoxicating.

In the days following the Mark incident, police came and investigated. They had their suspicions about me after talking to Mr. Goodwin. He noticed how the other kids respected and looked up to me like never before after the incident. But no one would talk, not even Mark. As bad as he was, he understood the code like everybody else. And since there was no smoking gun and no witness, there was no case. At the end of the day, as far as the authorities were concerned, it was just some bastard nigga that was cut up and so the case was eventually swept under the rug. Once Mark got out of the hospital, he was transferred to another home upstate and we never saw him again. Consequently, the boys voted me as Mark's replacement as Dorm Director. I was in charge for the first time in my life, and I liked it.

The years started flying by after that. One day kind of ran into the next thanks to Mr. Goodwin. Angry about the fact that he never found out what happened; Mr. Goodwin tried sticking it to us every chance he got, the bastard! We got the most work assignments, the most cleaning duties, and the least amount of recreational time. It didn't matter to us though. Just the fact that we could get a good night sleep without fear was worth it.

On top of that, life in an orphanage can be painfully mundane at times. You see the same handful of people every day. You eat the same nasty food for breakfast, lunch, and dinner. You watch the same programs on television, and play the same ole games at night. The only thing that broke the monotony, the only thing that gave me a little joy was my Pop's trumpet. Every now and then, I'd grab it, find me an isolated area, and practice my scales. On those rare occasions, I'd creep down to the library while everyone else was outside. They had this old-fashion turntable that I used to listen to the Miles Davis album Pop bought me. I spent hours trying to emulate his sound, and whenever I got close, it was one of the few things that brought a smile to my face.

By the time 1972 came around, I was sixteen and not so average anymore. I was over six-foot tall like my old man, but a bit more muscular. I even had a little peach fuzz growing on my upper lip. Mousey didn't change at all. He still looked like an over grown rat, but Frito, wow. He was massive. On a sunny day, if Frito stood between the sun and me, it felt like an eclipse. He'd grown into this intimidating and imposing figure although his face was still covered with freckles. Even though Frito was bigger, taller, and stronger, he still looked up to me.

Mitch and white boy Jake were transferred not too long after Mark left. Mr. Goodwin liked to shake thing up from time to time. A bunch of kids came and went to Dorm 6 over the years, but the only constant was Frito, Mousey, and me. So we had a special bond. Then in the summer of 72, we had two new fish that would further change my life forever.

I was summoned to Mr. Goodwin office as usual. Years had passed, but the frosty looks and contempt in his voice for me remained. Standing against the wall holding their bags was a white and black kid. Mr. Goodwin walked over and introduced them, "This is Dennis," he said pointing to the lanky black kid whose face was covered with acne, "And this is Peter," he said tapping the short white kid on the shoulder. Looking at him, I could immediately tell he was Italian. He had this long black curly hair and tanned skin like the Italians I use to see all the time back home in New York.

"This is Neil. He'll take you to where you'll be staying," Mr. Goodwin said as he turned and went back into his office.

Dennis strutted over to me with this cool ass

walk, "How's it hanging baby?" He dropped one of his bags and extended his hand while flashing this huge grin. I was amazed to say the least. No fish talks unless spoken to for at least the first few days. It takes that long to get over the initial shock of coming to this place.

"You gonna give me some skin or what baby?" he asked. I slid the palm of my hand over his as Peter watched impatiently waiting for me to show him to his bunk.

"My friends call me Denny. I'm from sunny South Dallas baby, where the sun always shines!" he proclaimed enthusiastically.

"Cool Denny, grab your things and follow me," I ordered. They followed me into the dorm and I showed them their bunks, as Frito and Mousey looked on. Peter neatly put away his clothes in his footlocker without saying a single word. He pulled out an Archie comic, sat on his bunk, and ignored the rest of us. Denny, on the other hand, carelessly tossed his bags under the bed and walked over toward Frito and Mousey.

"How's it hanging my brothers?" Denny said smoothly giving them skin also. They were stunned like me over his forwardness and upbeat attitude. "The name is Denny from sunny South Dallas baby, where the sun always shines!" he announced once again with such reverence and pride that you would've thought South Dallas was some fascinating exotic city on the same level as say Paris, Rome, or London.

"I'm from South Dallas too," Mousey responded. Even though he'd gotten a little older and hit puberty, his voice still shrieked like steam coming out of a tea kettle.

"Oh yeah, what part?"

"I used to live off Oakland Ave and Metropolitan, but that was long time ago. I've been here since I was eleven," Mousey shot back.

"I can dig it baby. Ain't too much changed since then, except they're bussing niggas to school with white kids now."

"Wow! So what landed you in here?" Mousey inquired.

"I got picked up on a B and E, and the fuzz found out I was living on my own. Actually, I lucked out. They had pity on me, the suckers. They sent me here instead of juvenile," Denny joked slapping Mousey on the shoulder.

"What happened to your folks?" Mousey asked.

"My mom died when I was little, and my old man is in prison for armed robbery. I've been on my own since I was about fourteen. But it's cool though, 'cause my other family looked out for me."

"Why you didn't go and stay with them.

Anywhere else is better than here," Mousey responded.

"I would if I could, but they're not my blood kin," Denny said falling on his bunk and kicking his feet up on the headboard.

"I don't get it. If they're not your kin, then what kind of family are they?" I said curiously sliding a little closer and leaning against the bed.

"I don't know if I can tell you," Denny said flashing this sly grin, "They like to keep a low profile."

"We can keep a secret! Ain't that right fellas?" Mousey said eagerly as his beady eyes darted back and forth between Frito and me. We nodded our heads in agreement.

"That's right, what goes down here stays here. That's the Dorm 6 code," Frito added folding his massive arms.

"Okay," Denny said sitting up in the bed. Signaling for us to move in closer, his eyes quickly scan the room again. He dropped his voice barely above a whisper, "Check it out. A few years ago, sunny South Dallas was like crazy. Niggas was acting a fool. Gangs were fighting over territories, junkies everywhere; it wasn't safe for a lady to walk the boulevard at night. Then this cold ass brother name Sheridan came along and created this crew called *the Dark Hand*. He organized the streets, put the gangs in line, and brought peace to the neighborhood. He put an end to all the bullshit killings and made it so that all of us niggas could get paid. He turned us into a tight family that fears no one, where everybody looks out for each other."

"Wow, so your crew is running things like that," Mousey asked in astonishment.

"I'm telling you baby, *the Dark Hand* runs everything in Dallas!"

"Everything," I repeated sitting up on my bed hanging on every word Denny said. I have to admit that I was intrigued from the very start, not really sure why. Maybe it was because of the family aspect and the possibility of acceptance that drew me in. Don't know. All I do know is he had my full attention.

"Everything!" Denny bragged grinning and hopping to his feet while getting extremely animated, "Shit, we control it all baby. Bitches, gambling, alcohol, anything you can imagine, even the police!"

"See, now that's what I'm talking about, some real niggas," Mousey said giving Denny some skin, "So how do you get down with them?"

"You got to show your loyalty and you got to show that you can make bread."

Denny had stirred up quite the interest in the *Dark Hand*. Over the following weeks, he'd go on and on about their exploits. From the time we rise, through lunch and dinner, he'd brag about how much money he was making, and how no one would dare fuck with them, not even the police. Frito, Mousey, and I would hang on his every word. To us, it was the answers to all our dreams. We were kids that got picked on and disrespected, and here was a kid talking about belonging to something that got the ultimate respect. We were kids who had nothing, and here was a kid talking about regular guys like us making big time loot. We were kids who society forgot and nobody wanted, and here was a kid talking about a crew who would accept us like brothers and have our backs. Yes, it's easy to see how Denny sucked us in.

The other new kid, Peter, maintained his silence. He would sit by himself in the cafeteria and eat alone. He'd sit alone and watch us play basketball during recess, and in the evening before bed, his face was buried in those Archie comics. It was a little weird but not uncommon or unexpected. The majority of the white boys didn't talk to us and we didn't talk to them either. Just because we were poor orphan kids, didn't mean we weren't immune to segregation.

One evening, after dinner, me and the guys were heading back to the dorm after another shitty dinner consisting of Meatloaf, peas, and lumpy mashed potatoes. Denny was bragging like always, as Frito was knocking down his customary bag of corn chips. Usually Peter followed behind us on our way back to the dorm, but this night he was nowhere to be found.

We stroll back into our dorm and I could see the lights were on in the bathroom. I didn't pay much attention at first until I heard what I thought was someone moaning. As Mousey and Frito collapsed on their bunks, Denny followed me to the bathroom. I tried to open the door, but it was locked. I pressed my ear against the door and once again, I heard another moan and the sound of a tussle. The lock on the door was like everything else in that place, old and outdated. I jiggled the doorknob for a few seconds and it popped right open.

I walked in to see Peter being held down by this kid name Cole from dorm 5. Cole was a big, black, greasy looking nigga that easily outweighed Peter by a hundred pounds. I'm telling you, I've seen skillets that weren't as black as Cole. With his and Peter's pants around their ankles, Cole used his massive hand to bend the squirming Peter over the toilet. Cole was doing his best to shove his Johnson into Pete's ass.

"Let him go!" I shouted angrily.

"I will, just close the door and give me a minute," Cole responded.

"I don't think you heard me," I said walking

over stone face. I snatched Peter from his grasp and pulled him behind me. Then I grabbed a fist full of Cole's nappy afro and started pounding his ass unmercifully. He fell to the floor and curled up like a fetus. That's when I started kicking that fool with everything I had. I don't know what came over me; I was like a man possessed. The more I kicked him, the more I wanted to kick. In some strange way, it wasn't Cole I was unleashing my venom on, it was Mark. I could hear the commotion behind me as Frito came barreling through the door. He and Denny wrestled me away from Cole.

"Get your shit and get the fuck out my dorm!" I yelled as I started to snap out of it.

Still curled up in fetal position, Cole rolled around on the ground moaning in pain and holding his ribs. Lying on the floor with his pants still around his ankles, he wiped the blood from his nose. Scrambling to get back to his feet, Cole quickly pulled his pants up and fastened his belt, "What's your fucking problem man?"

"You're my problem! You want to bust a nut, grab some Vaseline, and beat your meat like everyone else."

Without saying another word, Cole lowered his head, grabbed his side in pain, and slithered out of the door and down the hall. I turned my attention back to Peter. He straightened his self out, and was trying to shake off the shock of what just happen. "You okay man?" I asked.

"Fine," Peter snapped as he turned and quickly exited the bathroom.

"Damn! You almost fuck that kid up," Denny commented.

"I don't play that shit in here," I replied as I grabbed a towel from the rack to wipe Cole's blood off my fist.

Denny stepped back with his hands up in the air, "You don't have to worry about me baby, I like pussy holes, not assholes," he joked.

Not amused, I continued over to the faucet and washed my hands thoroughly. It was difficult to get Cole's blood out of the grooves of my knuckles. Once Frito saw that everything was cool, he walked back into the other room. Denny, on the other hand, casually glided over behind me. He tried to be friendly and slid his arm around my shoulder.

"Don't touch me," I snapped pulling away. Although years had gone by since the whole Mark fiasco, the thought of someone touching me still made my skin crawl.

"Sorry baby! Didn't mean nothing by it," Denny said grinning as he stepped back. Folding his arms, he casually leaned against the wall real cool like, "I see that you know how to handle yourself, take charge."

"What's it to you?"

"Easy baby, eeeeeasy, I'm on your side. Just letting you know I like the way you took care of that little situation. You put that punk in his place."

"Really?"

"Hell yeah! That fool deserved that ass whipping. You don't mess with another man like that," Denny said turning toward the mirror and checking out his teeth to make sure they were clean. He cut his eyes at the door to make sure the coast was clear, "You know what I was telling you about the *Dark Hand* was true, and they could use a strong brother like you on the outside."

I immediately perked up, "You think so?"

"Oh, I know so. You're exactly the kind of brother they're looking for. Look here, I only got a couple of months before I turn eighteen and I'm out of here. When you get out, you look me up and I'll take you under my wing and school you to the game."

A few days went by and things returned to normal, sort of. Thanks to Denny, word had spread like wild fire of the ass whipping I gave Cole. Now, not only was I respected in my own dorm, but the entire building. Kids who never said two words to me were coming up shaking my hand, begging to be my friend. Boys from other dorms would volunteer to clean my room and make my bed. At lunch, kids offered me their food. Once again, I must admit, being respected was a wonderful feeling.

Up to that point, the only person that hadn't come up to me was Peter. He still mainly kept to his self, especially after what transpired. That is until one sunny afternoon on the playground. The boys were playing basketball, as usual on a Saturday. While they were on the blacktop, I slipped away to a secluded corner with a little shade to block out the sun. I took out Pop's horn and held it tightly against my chest before playing it as I customarily do. I always started out playing a cord in A-sharp, it put me in a sentimental mood, reminded me of New York. I could picture the Manhattan skyline with every note I played. Then as I played Louis Armstrong's *What A Wonderful World,* Peter came strolling up to me with his hands in his pockets whistling along the same tune.

"You play pretty good," Peter commented, as the sun reflected off his dark brown eyes. His skin had grown darker since the summer began. The heat of Texas can do that to you. It made him look more Greek or Spanish than Italian.

"Thanks."

"Where you learn to play?"

"My old man taught me. He used to play."

"Cool! Look, about the other day. I just wanted to say thanks for looking out for me," Peter said kicking the gravel under his feet while cracking his knuckles. "I ah…"

"Don't mention it," I said cutting him off. I could tell he was embarrassed. I know how difficult it was to talk about, to think about. If he's anything like me, he probably relives the experience every night!

Peter had fire in his eyes as he grinded his teeth, "You can best believe I'm going to take care of that punk, when the time is right. Nobody fucks with Peter Marcello and gets away with it!"

"Marcello, Marcello why does that name sound familiar?" I commented scratching my head,

"You probably heard of my uncle, Victor Marcello, the boss of New Orleans.

"Yeah, that right. He's been all over the news the last few months. They've been trying to deport him, right?"

"Right. How you know about that?"

"Eh, this place can get boring. So from time to time, I read the paper. It's the only way to keep in touch with the outside world. So Victor Marcello is your uncle, huh?" I was skeptical to say the least. Every kid in here has some sort of special story of who he is, where they're from, and who they're related to. And most often, it's bullshit.

"That's right."

"So why are you here?"

"I was out here with my old man while he was taking care of some business. He was picked by the cops for a job he did a few years back, and they gave him ten years in the pen. My mother died right after I was born. So now, my uncle is working on getting me out here. He can't come himself 'cause they're trying to say he's not a legal citizen."

"Well Peter, you're a part of Dorm 6 now, and we're like brothers around here. We look out for each other, no matter what." I wiped off the trumpet with a soft, dry rag and carefully placed it back in the case. I walked over to Peter and extended my hand in friendship.

"Hmm," he mumbled mulling it over, rubbing his hand across his strong jaw line. Peter curiously looked around for a moment. Finally, he took my hand and shook it firmly, "My friends call me Pete."

"Okay, Pete," I said flashing a slight grin. I liked Pete right away, didn't matter to me that he was Italian. He was cool and we all accepted him as one of us. The boys of Dorm 6 had a shared experience that transcended racial barriers, and brought us all closer together.

My father's voice started cracking and he began to cough violently. All the talking made his throat parched. He summed up what little strength he had to sit up in his hospital bed. He looked around for some water, but it was difficult for him to see because he was still a little groggy.

Sister Simmons, shocked by what she just heard, sat up straight in her chair like she was in a trance. Her hazel eyes were completely glazed over, and a few seconds went by before she snapped back to reality. The sound of my father knocking over a plastic cup and his loud coughing finally snapped her out of it. "I'm sorry, let me get you something to drink," Sister Simmons commented. Picking up the cup, she gingerly walked over to the sink. Although she's young in spirit and enthusiasm, the arthritis in her joints has taken its toll on her seventy-eight year old body. She rinsed out the glass and brought him some fresh water as quick as she could.

Bruce, who was still guarding my father's room along with Earl, cracked the door and stuck his head in, "Excuse me sir, but the doctor would like to see you."

The old man lifted his hand and motioned that it was okay to let him in. Dr. Anderson, a rather average looking middle age white man, nervously made his way into the room. It was obvious that Bruce and Earl, who can be quite intimidating, had the poor doctor shaken up. He quickly began checking my father's vital signs.

"Mr. Wright, how are we doing this evening?" Dr. Anderson asked while scanning over my father's chart trying to keep his hands from shaking.

"How do you think?"

"Yeah, right. I see that you're running low on your morphine drip. I'll have the nurse bring you some more."

"No."

"Excuse me," Dr. Anderson replied wearing a confused look.

"Look here doc, we both know I don't have long to live. So I don't want to waste what few moments I have left drugged up," the old man said between coughs, "Right now, me being lucid is more important than the pain."

"I see. Okay, well I'll be back to check on you later," Dr. Anderson said as he swiftly darted out the door.

While the door was cracked, the old man

called out for Bruce. Bruce poked his head in once again, "Yes sir."

"I'm not to be disturbed again, for any reason, not even my son."

"Yes sir," he replied closing the door.

He turned his attention back to Sister Simmons, who handed him the cup of water. "Thank you," he said taking a sip.

Sitting back down in the chair across from my father, Sister Simmons shook her head while rubbing her hands together, "So you're Neil Wright?"

"Yep."

"The Neil Wright, the gangster I read about in the papers?"

"In the flesh."

"And you're from New York?"

"That's right."

"My God," she said taking a deep breath. I ah…I don't know what to say."

"What's there to say sister? I make no apologies for who I am. I had to do what I had to do to survive."

"I know, and like I said I'm not here to judge you, but you should've never been in that situation. Your mother should have been there for you."

My father just chuckled at that comment, "My mother is a worthless bitch!"

"You don't really mean that."

"The hell I don't! If it weren't for her selfish ass, my father would still be alive. There's no doubt in my mind!" my father replied squirming around in his bed feeling a bit agitated.

"Did that Mrs. Walker, did she continue to look for her?"

"Probably, but how can you find someone that don't wanna be found?"

"Maybe she didn't look in the right place."

"I really don't give a damn where she looked. If my mother was any kind of a woman, she should've come looking for me. She should've left an address or phone number or something, damn it!"

"You're right," Sister Simmons murmured bowing her head. She stood up and began pacing back and forth at the foot of his bed with fingers sliding against the hand railing. What you've been through, it's horrible!"

"I've only scratched the surface sister," my father said taking another swig of water, "You haven't heard shit yet!"

I woke up from a rare goodnight sleep to find that I was surrounded by Pete, Frito, and Mousey. All three stood there with their hands on their hips staring at me with stone faces. Then without warning, they quickly converged on me and began tickling me unmercifully.

"Stop playing!" I shouted as I laughed loudly while twisting and turning trying to avoid their probing fingers. I was extremely ticklish back then.

"Happy birthday bro!" Frito blurted out as he finally stopped tickling me.

"So what does it feel like to officially be a man today?" Pete asked.

"Fuck that, what does it feel like to finally get out this bitch?" Mousey joked.

"Wonderful boys, wonderful," I said grinning while hopping to my feet with my chest poked out.

"Damn! First Denny, now you, I can't wait until I turn eighteen, so I be out of here too," Frito commented.

"You got to be grown like me first, blood," I

joked licking my index fingers and stroking my mustache and eyebrows.

"So you know where you're going first when you get out of here?" Frito asked plopping his big ass down on my bed, munching on corn chips again as I started getting dressed.

"The first thing I'm gonna do is get some flowers and visit my old man's grave. The next thing I'm gonna do is catch the first train to New York City," I replied beaming with excitement, "I'm finally going home!"

The room quickly fell quiet as the familiar sound of squeaky sneakers echoing down the hallway suddenly approached our dorm. Mr. Goodwin strolled in wearing a t-shirt and dungarees with his long hair flapping in the breeze. Although years had gone by, the contempt he had for me was still evident. He stopped short at the door and leaned against the wall.

"Mr. Wright, you need to get your things together. We're leaving for the bus station in thirty minutes," Mr. Goodwin announced tapping his cheap wristwatch.

I didn't respond to him, not one word, not even a gesture. I quit doing it a long time ago. He had no respect for me, and the feeling was mutual. He eventually turned and left the room once he saw me pull out my duffle bag that was already packed.

"Forget about his ass!" Frito snarled as he sat up in my bed, "How you gonna go off to New York without me? What about our plans? You know getting a place, joining the *Dark Hand*, making some major bread."

"I ain't forgot bro," I said giving Frito a Dorm 6 handshake that we invented. That's when we grabbed each other's forearm with our right hand, slid down the arm to shake hands, snap fingers simultaneously, and then did this smooth slide like the Temptations. "I'm gonna be out here taking care of business until you get out a year from now. Don't worry about a thing, Rupert."

"I told you about calling me that. I should've never told you my real name," Frito shot back, as a smile spread across his chubby, freckled filled face. He breathed easier as I calmed his concerns. I slung my duffle bag over my shoulder and grabbed my Pop's horn case. It was a bittersweet moment. I was jubilant inside with the thought of leaving the place. It's been six long, long, long years since I first arrived, and the only thing I've had to look forward to was getting out and going home. I literately marked the days on my calendar every morning. On the other hand, I was fighting back the tears. Frito, Pete, and Mousey were like family to me, and I was going to miss them.

I walked over to Mousey next. We stared

at each other for a moment. Then I gave him a Dorm 6 handshake as well, "Brothers for life," I said.

"Brothers for life," Mousey repeated.

I walked over to Pete next. Pete's short ass had to look up at me to lock eyes. I think my man quit growing when he was about thirteen. I gave him the handshake as well, "Brothers for life."

"Brothers for life," Pete repeated. They followed me down the hall and to the front door. That was as far as Mr. Goodwin would let them go. As I got on the bus, I took one last look back to see the guys standing there like lost puppy dogs waiting for their owners to return.

———

I stepped out of the bus station in downtown Dallas on chilly afternoon with my bags, two hundred dollars cash in my pockets and a referral to a transition house. I stood on the corner for a moment taking in my surroundings. It was amazing how much Dallas had changed in six years. The skyline looked amazing with these fancy looking glass buildings. I watched as the multitudes of people walked the streets while drinking coffee and reading newspapers. I listened as I heard the sound of police sirens, engines running, and horns blowing. I took a deep breath of that familiar city air filled with car exhaust, fumes from food cooking, and cigarette smoke. I almost forgot what it was like to walk the streets, the smells, the sounds. I missed it. I noticed these strange stares and some snickering by the people passing by, but I didn't give a damn. I stood on that corner twirling around like Mary Tyler Moore. Without thinking, I dropped my things, raised my arms to the heavens and yelled at the top of my voice, "I'm free!"

My plan was to get a room for the night, go see my Pop, and hop on the next train for New York. I walked a couple of blocks and saw a motel with the vacancy sign flashing and a ten-dollar a night room rate. I strolled into the lobby that smelled like stale socks and walked up to the middle-aged white man who was wearing reading glasses glancing over a rolled up newspaper.

"Excuse me sir, can my kind stay here?" I politely inquired.

His eyes peaked up from his newspaper for a second then he went back to reading, "Is your money green?"

"Yes sir."

"Then your kind can stay here."

So I paid him, got my key, and dropped my things off in my room. I went to the nearest grocery store and picked up a dozen daisies. They were Pop's favorite. He loved the smell of fresh daisies. Summer wouldn't begin until Pop got some daisies, crack the window, and put them on the window seal.

I caught the bus to Potter's Field Cemetery and walked around looking at each wooden marker until I found the one with Pop's name on it. It looked like nobody had been there since the day my old man was buried. It looked like nobody came period. There were no flowers on any of the graves. Weeds had taken over and killed most of the grass. There was trash everywhere. I kneeled down and cleaned the debris from around his grave, "Hey Pop, I told you I'd be back. Look what I got," I said placing the flowers neatly next to the rotted piece of wood that had my old man's name carved in it, "I brought your favorite, daisies. I miss you so much. Don't worry, I'm going to get you out of this nasty place, and put you somewhere really nice. You'll see. Look what I brought with me." I opened up the case and pulled out his horn. The night before I left I spent most of the evening polishing it, until it sparkled like new.

"I've been practicing," I said enthusiastically putting my lips on the mouthpiece and playing a few notes of Miles Davis' *So What.* "Not bad huh, Pop?" I chuckled, "Not as good as you, but you know." I commented as I put the horn back in the box, pulled out the only picture I had left of him and me, and took a seat next to his grave,

"I'm going to finish what you started by coming here. One day, soon, I'll be rich and powerful. I'm going to make you proud of me, Pop."

<hr/>

I figured since I was only going to be in town for one more night, I looked up a familiar friend, Denny. So I caught the bus to South Dallas not really having a true destination in mind, only remembering that Denny said that was his hangout area and that everyone knew him over there. The bus let me off on Forest Ave, right in front of the Forest Theater. The first thing I saw when I stepped off the bus was the huge marquee advertising a double feature, The Godfather II and Death Wish, for a dollar. Forest Ave was definitely the heart of South Dallas, the main artery that ran through this community. I looked down the block and saw that the street ran right into the State Fair of Texas. The famous Cotton Bowl and a massive Ferris wheel with Texas written on it, could be seen from a mile away. As I strolled down the avenue, passing by numerous people as they shopped or going about their business, I noticed an old fashion barbershop sandwiched between a liquor store and a meat market. I thought to myself *what the hell* and decided to go in and try there first. It was as good a place as any to start my search.

It was a Tuesday afternoon, so the place was empty; there was only one guy in a chair getting his head cut. The other barbers were standing around talking shit drowning out the fact that Roberta Flack was singing *Killing Me Softly* on the radio. You must thought I was Muhammad Ali or something, because when I walked in the room, everyone immediately stopped what they were doing and stared directly at me with their mouths wide open.

"Goddamn! You step out a time machine from the sixties or something boy? I ain't seen threads like these, since Jackie Wilson was on the Ed Sullivan Show!" One barber joked while looking me up and down. The other guys broke out in laughter. I never really paid much attention to my clothes before. I wore what they gave me at the orphanage, hand-me-downs mostly. I didn't have much of a choice. As I scan their clothes and saw them wearing the latest style, bell-bottoms and butterfly collar shirts. My eyes looked closely at my own clothes for the first time and I saw just how different I was dressed.

"Damn, is it raining outside, 'cause you definitely ready for a flood," another barber joked tugging on my pants.

"You had to dig deep in your old man's closet to find a shirt that old," yet another guy added laughing hysterically, "With them old clothes you got on, you don't need a haircut you need conk. Where's the lye and potatoes at?" He mocked licking his fingers and pretending to slick back his hair.

An older gentleman stood up from his chair smiling, "Don't mind them. How can I help you brother?"

"I'm looking for a friend of mines. His name is Denny, tall, lanky, dark skin," I said motioning with my hands to show his height.

"Denny, Denny," the man said snapping his fingers trying to place the name.

"He's talking about motor-mouth," joked the one guy getting his hair cut.

"Oh yeah, motor-mouth. He stays up the street in those apartments off Grand Ave."

"Motor-mouth, we talking about the same guy?" I asked with an inquisitive look.

"Tall, thin, runs his mouth like the motor on my car outside," the older gentleman joked pointing to a sixty nine Impala parked out front.

"I see. Thanks for the info. How do I get there from here?" I asked.

"I'm about to leave and I'm heading that way. I'll give you a lift. The name is Otis," he said shaking my hand.

"Neil. I appreciate that."

"Don't mention it. Before we go, why don't you let me cut you up? I can't do anything about those clothes, but at least I can bring your haircut into the seventies," Otis offered, brushing the hair clippings from his barber chair.

So I sat down and took him up on his offer. He shaped me up real nice, had my afro as round as a globe. We slipped into his ride and headed up the block. Otis was cool, but he annoyed me with all the small talk. He pulled into these raggedy looking apartments that were littered with cigarette butts and empty beer cans. A bunch of hardheads were out front listening to music and passing around a fifth of thunderbird.

"You know which apartment he stays in?" I said cracking open the door.

"No, but I'm sure one of those fellows could tell you," Otis responded looking at the hardheads.

"Thanks." I slammed the door and approached the guys who were sitting on the steps. They all turned toward me and started elbowing each other.

"Checkout blood," one guy said standing up and setting the bottle of thunderbird on the ground.

"What the fuck you got on nigga!" another guy said giggling uncontrollably.

"I think you in the wrong neighborhood blood," said another guy with big crusty lips who looked to be the leader of the bunch. They walked over and started forming a circle around me. Their approach concerned me. They didn't look like the neighborhood greeting party. I was mentally preparing for the fight though. Between the barbershop and these knuckleheads, I had about enough of the jokes. I had made up in my mind that the next fool to say something was going to be the first one to get knocked out. Then I heard in the distance.

"Neil?" I immediately recognize the voice. I looked around and saw Denny in a red robe wearing a pair of dark shades standing at the top of the stairs with a hand full of mail. "Neil is that you baby?"

"Yeah."

"Get your ass up here boy!" Denny commanded with this huge grin. Obviously, Denny had some pull. The demeanor of the knuckleheads surrounding me quickly changed. They wiped the silly grins from their faces and backed up. I stared them down as I walked past them with my chest out just to let them know that I was not to be fucked with. I knifed my way through the crowd and up the stairs to Denny.

"What's happening baby?" Denny reached like he was going to hug me, but when he saw me draw back, I think he immediately remembered I didn't like being touched. So he gave me a spirited Dorm 6 handshake. "Come on in."

I followed him into his place and took a seat on the couch. The apartment was as big as shoebox. The furniture was old; the couch had a piece of scotch tape on one of the edges, holding it together. But to my surprise, his pad was immaculately clean. Back at the dorm, I can remember Denny being nasty and never putting up his clothes, so you can imagine how stunned I was.

"Damn Baby, what the hell you got on?" Denny asked taking off his shades to reveal his bloodshot eyes that scanned me up and down.

"It's all that I had," I replied shrugging my shoulders.

"You can't walk the streets like that. We got to get you some new threads, especially if you gonna be hanging with me. I got a reputation to uphold," Denny joked putting the shades back on. He went into his bedroom and came out with a decent outfit under his arm, "Here, you can wear this until we get you some new digs. So when you get out?" he asked plopping down on the couch as his robe swung open to reveal his stripped colored boxers. Reaching under the coffee table, Denny pulled out a shoebox that was full of marijuana and a package of *one point fives* wrapping paper.

"I got out this morning. My first taste of freedom in a long time, I love it," I said smiling rubbing my stomach, "So, what are you doing?"

"I'm rolling a joint baby," he said licking the paper and putting the final touches on a nice fat joint, "That's right; you've never had one. You wanna taste?"

"Nah, that's okay."

"You sure, 'cause this is some good shit?"

"Nah I'm cool."

Denny shrugged his shoulders, lit the joint, and took a long drag. "Hey bitch, you wanna hit of this!" he yelled.

Strolling out of the bedroom was a pretty, caramel-skin girl with long braided hair. She had a shapely hourglass figure that was only covered by a long white t-shirt. She sat on the edge of the couch, next to Denny, and took a hit off the joint after Denny took another one first.

"This is my main man Neil. Neil, this is my bitch, Rhonda," he said slapping her on her enormous ass. Rhonda, acting real shy, just smiled at me halfheartedly and waived. I watched as Denny and Rhonda passed the joint back and forth a couple of more times before she turned and left.

"Fine ain't she?" Denny asked grinning as we both watched her ass bounce as she sashayed her way to the bedroom, "She can cook her ass off too. You hungry? You want me to have her fix you up a little something?"

"Nah I'm fine."

"So, if you like me, you didn't go to that bullshit transition house. So where are you staying?"

"In a motel downtown."

"Not anymore baby. Get your things you're staying with me. Me casa is su casa."

"It don't matter. I'm leaving for New York tomorrow."

"Really? You got bread like that?"

"I got the money they gave me when I got out."

"That funky little two hundred dollars, that ain't about shit. You know how high the cost of living is these days. The rent here is a damn near a hundred dollars a month, and I'll bet you in a city like New York; it's twice that much. You haven't been there in years. What you gonna do for money when you get there? Where you gonna stay? Who do you know after all these years?"

I sat there mulling over everything that Denny was hitting me with. I didn't think about any of those things. I was so happy to be out. I just wanted to go and throw caution to the wind, but he was right. I hadn't been there in years; I had no money, and who knows if the people I knew when I was a kid were still around. Denny saw my confused looked and leaned closer.

"Check it out baby; you know I've been working on a few things since I got out, and I could use a brother like you to help me get my shit popping. I was serious when I told you about the *Dark Hand*. I got the connections baby. I'm in there. I'm this close to becoming a member," he said with his index finger and thumb only an inch apart, "Once I'm in, you're in. You stay with me a year or so, and I'll guarantee you'll have more money than you'll know what to do with. Then you can go back to the big apple in style and take a bit out of that bitch!"

"Okay," I said enthusiastically remembering how much I wanted to be a part of the *Dark Hand* family. Besides, I had no other options. "So what did you have in mind?"

"You ever heard of the pigeon drop?"

CHAPTER 15
FEBRUARY 12 1974

I woke up to the smell of biscuits baking, grits boiling on the stove, and the sound of bacon frying. As my eyes focused from the sunlight's glare through the living room window, I saw Rhonda in the kitchen hovering over the stove in her panties and a long t-shirt fixing breakfast. I know I wasn't supposed to look, but I couldn't help it. She had the perfect ass that was so massive, that the white t-shirt she had on didn't quite cover it.

So I bunked on their couch, which was actually more comfortable then my old broken-down bunk at the dorm. When I flipped through the channels on Denny's nineteen inch black and white television last night, with a pair of pliers because of the broken knobs, I noticed how paper thin the walls were. I could hear every little sound throughout the apartment, including Rhonda yelling, "Fuck me daddy, fuck me daddy!" while the brass headboard banged against the wall. Lucky for me Denny fucked like a rabbit, so the whole thing was usually over in about three to five minutes. It was cool though; cause no matter how many times they fooled around through the night, Rhonda was up at the crack of dawn cooking Denny and me breakfast. I was amazed to say the least. The girl had stamina.

This morning I was a little nervous because it was the day we were going to execute Denny's score. Denny came strolling out of the room impeccably dressed. He had those dark shades on of course, but something about him was different. He seemed incredibly energetic, and his nose was redder the Rudolf's on Christmas Eve. Plopping down on the couch next to me, he kicked his feet up on the coffee table.

"You ready to do this baby?" he asked between sniffles.

"Sure."

"Good, just remember to stick with the plan," he said flashing a cheesy grin while digging into his pocket and coming out with this huge roll of money with a rubber band around it. He casually tossed it in my lap, "Check it out baby! This is my finest work."

"Damn! I thought you didn't have any bread. Where did this come from?"

He laughed, and then commanded, "Open it up."

I took off the rubber band and unfolded the stack money to see newspapers that were cut into the same shape of money.

"It's called a Philadelphia roll. I was up all night making it just right. Well, maybe not all night. Ain't that right bitch?" Denny joked, creeping over and smacking Rhonda on her ass again just as she was putting the food on the table.

We quickly ate breakfast, which was fantastic as usual, and darted out the door. The bus was pulling up to the bus stop, just as we came down the flight of stairs. We yelled and waived our arms wildly while sprinting across the parking lot trying to flag down the bus driver before he pulled away. Working up a sudden sweat, we climbed into bus and plopped down in the first seats we saw.

"Remember, keep your distance. Wait for the sign, I'm gonna tug on my collar when I start talking to the mark. Don't take the first offer; wait until the guy is almost ready to walk away before you finally give in. You got it?" Denny asked as his eyes constantly darted back and forth while he frequently continued to sniffle and rub his nose.

"I got it. I'm just wondering why can't I be the smooth-talking guy with the money making the pitch." I inquired.

"Like I told you before, you look too young. You barely got any facial hair. Plus I got the charisma, I got the salesmanship, and I've done it before baby, so I got the experience," Denny retorted adjusting his shades and cap. He glanced at his reflection on the back of one of the metal seats while smiling and checking his teeth. "How they look? Are they nice and white?" he asked.

"Your teeth are fine," I sighed.

After about a twenty-minute ride, we hopped off the bus on the corner of Hampton and Ledbetter in a neighborhood of well-to-do blacks called Oak Cliff. Denny got off the bus first and started walking to the Westcliff Mall. I lingered behind and watch from a distance as he made his way toward one of the shops. A flower stand had a large assortment of plants placed neatly along the sidewalk as patrons browsed through the inventory. As one of the customers started asking the owner questions trying to make up their mind between tulips or violets, Denny snuck to the side, pulled a woman's watch from his pocket, and carefully hid it among the plants while the owner wasn't looking. By the time the owner finished with the customer, Denny was pretending to be frantically looking for something.

"Excuse me, can I help you sir?" asked the owner, a clean-shaven white man with bags under his green eyes as if he hadn't slept in weeks.

"Yeah, I'm looking for a watch. I think I accidentally dropped it somewhere around here," Denny replied putting on a performance worthy of an Academy Award as he lifted, poked, and prodded numerous flowers, "You haven't seen it have you?"

"I'm afraid not," the owner said joining in on the search.

"Damn! It's my mother's watch passed down from her mother, a family heirloom. She's going to kill me if I don't find it. I was supposed to be bringing it up here to get it cleaned at the jewelry store," Denny stated now on his knees looking for the watch.

"Well I tell you what; I'll keep an eye out for it," the owner reached into his pocket, whipped out a pencil, and grabbed an old receipt from the register, "Here, write down your name and number and if I find or if someone turns it in, I'll give you a call."

"Man, I appreciate that, and look here, I'm willing to offer a reward," Denny said pulling out the Philadelphia roll and flashing it in front of the guy.

"A reward?" the owner asked with eyes wide open starting at the roll.

"Yeah, at least hundred dollars," Denny added while gently tugging on the collar of his shirt, giving me my cue.

"I'll definitely keep my eyes open," the owner said taking the paper that Denny scribbled a fake number on, and then shaking his hand vigorously.

I waited a good thirty minutes after Denny

walked away before I approached the stand. I'm amazed how calm I was. I casually strolled over and started looking at a plant as if I was going to buy one. As I scan over the flowers, I made my way over to the one that Denny planted the watch under.

"Wow!" I said loud enough to catch the attention of the store owner. He swiftly made his way over to me.

"Excuse me, but did you just find that?"

"Yeah."

"Somebody was looking for that watch," the owner said looking on eagerly.

"Well, like my momma said, finder's keepers."

"Hold on a minute there kid. I'll tell you what, I'll give you five bucks for the watch," he offered, pulling his wallet out of his back pocket.

"I don't know much about jewelry, but this watch looks like it's worth way more than five bucks to me," I replied dangling it in front of him.

"Okay, how about twenty bucks?" he offered once again.

"I don't think so."

"How about forty bucks?"

"I don't know man," I responded glossing over it one last time.

"Alright kid...here's sixty dollars. Now that's a lot of cash for a kid like you," he said as he pulled out all the cash he had in his wallet,

"There's no one who's going to give you more than this for that watch."

"Oh, okay," I said taking the money while handing him the watch simultaneously.

That first score was just a tip of the iceberg. We hit several more scores that day. All told, we made an easy grand in a few hours without lifting a finger, but that was the easy part.

About a week went by before Denny took me with him to meet the headman himself, the infamous Mr. Sheridan. I heard so much about the man over the years that he began to take the persona of a folk hero. I couldn't believe how much power, clout and influence this man had in the community. Sheridan was like a ghetto superstar, a street legend, a man worthy of the highest respect. His very name was spoken with reverence by the people of South Dallas.

We strolled up to the front of Roscoe's Rack Room. It was Sheridan's unofficial head quarters. A little pool hall off Carroll Ave. where Sheridan kept an office in back. He'd routinely met with his soldiers there every afternoon. Denny was pumped up about the meeting. He wanted so badly to make a good impression, that the day before we went to Montgomery Wards to get some new threads just for the occasion. But I knew there could possibly be trouble, when just after breakfast, I saw him taking a hit off a joint. Denny was a motor-mouth sober, when he's high, shit, not only does he talk too much, but he's bound to put his foot in his mouth. Denny stopped just short of the door and started straightening his clothes and adjusting his hat one last time.

"I look okay," he asked.

"How many times you gonna keep asking me the same question. You look fine," I snapped slightly annoyed. He'd asked Rhonda and me the same fucking question all morning.

"How about my teeth?" he said picking at them. "They clean?"

"What is this obsession with your teeth? Every damn day, everywhere we go; you're asking about your fucking teeth!"

"My father always told me to take care of my teeth, keep them nice and clean. He said you can tell a lot about a person from their smile."

"Whatever," I said shrugging my shoulders.

"Blow it off if you want baby, but you're gonna wish you did like me when you have a mouth full cavities by the time your forty and I'm still walking around with a perfect smile." Denny said as he slid his tongue across the front of his teeth, fixed his shades on his face, and smiled at me, "Now when we get inside let me do all the talking. I know these guys. I know how they operate. Okay?"

"Sure, whatever you say. I still don't see why we're giving him all our money. I thought we were supposed to be trying to join his crew so that we could make money."

"Like I told you, we're giving him this money as a tribute, like a show of respect for the ability to use his name. That's how it works. We have to show that we can earn on our own. We have to show that we're worthy. Then when we do, he'll reward us with bigger and better gigs. You follow me?"

"I guess."

"Now you're sure I look okay?"

"You look fucking beautiful! Can we go in already?"

Making our way down the sidewalk, we were almost ran over by three kids sprinting by us yelling at the top of their lungs, "Nickel Willie, Nickel Willie!"

Standing at the phone booth on the corner, about to make a call, was an old man well dressed in a gray three-piece suit and matching fedora. Using a mahogany cane with a round brass tip to help him walk, the clean-shaven gentleman appeared to be a very friendly old man, as he flashed this sweet grin to the kids approaching. "Hello kiddies, what are you guys doing running around here?"

"Nickel Willie can we get some change for candy?" The three boys asked in unison.

"I don't know. Have you been good boys,

obeying your parents?" the old man asked jingling the change in his pocket.

"Yes!"

"You guys doing good in school?"

"Yes!"

"Ok, well here's a little something." He reached into his pocket and put a quarter's worth of nickels in each kids begging hand. "Now what do you say?"

"Thank you Nickel Willie," they all said as the turned and sprinted toward the small grocery store on the corner.

Denny stopped in his tracks and grabbed me by the shirt, "You know who that is?"

"Some nice old man," I responded shrugging my shoulders.

"Man, that's Nickel Willie, blood! A STONE-COLD KILLER! They say that man has killed so many people, they named a cemetery after him."

"That old man?" I asked with a raised eyebrow.

"Yes! I heard that when Nickel Willie found out that his old lady was cheating on him, he caught the guy and made an example of his ass. He strung him up naked from a telephone pole, cut of his dick and stuck it in his own ass to let niggas know that his wife was off limits. Shit, to this day, niggas treat his wife like Medusa from *Clash of the Titans*, when you see her, look the other fucking way."

We approached the front door and pushed it open and a cloud of cigarette smoke came oozing out. I had virgin lungs, so I naturally started coughing. A man holding a newspaper, leaning against a cigarette machine in the lobby looked at Denny and me rather peculiarly.

"What do you boys need?" he asked rudely.

"We're here to see Mr. Sheridan," Denny quickly responded rather confidentially.

"Is he expecting you?"

"Yes sir."

The man looked us up and down one more time. "Turn around," he commanded. We both looked at each other and then promptly followed his orders. He came up behind me, pushed me up against the wall, and began patting me down. After doing the same to Denny, he said, "Follow me."

He led us into the dimly lit pool hall. The place definitely had an old-fashioned feel to it. Even the music was old; I think Louis Jordan's *Beans and Cornbread* was playing on the jukebox. We passed by numerous tables where several guys, all with cigarettes dangling from their mouths, were scattered throughout. Some were shooting some stick. Others were drinking and conversing. It was a very laid-back atmosphere. We got to the back near the bar where three guys were sitting at a card table. One was a fat dark-skinned nigga with a mustache like Lamont from *Sanford and Son.* The other was Nickel Willie, who had just passed by us while we were being patted down. Nickel Willie was sipping a cup of coffee with one hand while holding a set of dominoes in the other mulling over his next play.

"Come on Nick, I've been waiting an eternity for you to play already!" the baldheaded brother barked.

"I don't know why you want to rush an ass whipping, but here you go. Twenty! That's game," Nickel Willie said slamming down a domino.

Suddenly, we heard an agitated voice from behind the paper, "Do you believe this Patty Hearst bullshit? This white bitch is richer than a Kennedy, and she's out here robbing banks like she's fucking Jesse James. I'll bet you when they finally catch up to her white ass, she won't do a day in jail. Meantime, these pigs out here would throw our black asses in jail in a heartbeat just for a damn speeding ticket."

"Right on," both guys replied as the bald brother shuffled the dominoes for the next game.

"Excuse me Skipper, got a couple of guys here to see you," said the guy who led us over.

The man who was reading the newspaper lowered it just enough that all we could see was his dark-brown eyes peeping over the top, "What can I do for you boys?"

Denny looked at me and took a step forward, "Afternoon Mr. Sheridan. I'm Denny, and uh… this is my friend Neil. I ah, I'm a friend of Locke, been doing some errands for him, trying to show my worth to him, to you, and this family. He told me that you were always on the lookout for new people. So I'm just looking for that opportunity. I'm a hard worker willing to make any sacrifices necessary, and to prove that, I wanted to come see you personally and show you my gratitude," Denny said as he reached into his pocket, pulled out the cash, and attempted to hand it to Mr. Sheridan.

"What are you doing?" Mr. Sheridan asked dropping the paper on the table. I was surprised at what I saw. From everything I heard about him and his reputation, I was expecting Superfly, Al Capone, Humphrey Bogart, a tough looking gangster in a pinstriped suit with a cigar, and a hat tilted to the side. I expected pinky rings, gold chains, and a nasty scare across his face. Maybe I watch too many gangster flicks. I don't know. But Mr. Sheridan was the antitheist of that. He was conservatively dressed in slacks, a navy blue turtleneck sweater, and a plaid blazer. No Jewelry! He had this neatly trimmed goatee and a small afro with a touch of gray sprinkled in. He pushed up a pair of black horn-rimmed glasses that were concealed by the paper to get a better look at Denny.

"Well... I thought it was okay to give you this," Denny stammered as his eyes darted back and forth between the three men sitting at the table who stopped playing dominoes and were all staring at him coldly.

"You thought," Mr. Sheridan mocked, "Do me a favor, take those glasses off, last time I checked, there's no sun in here." Denny quickly yanked his shades off and stuffed them in his jacket.

Sheridan made eye contact while sitting on the edge of his seat, "Let me tell you a story kid. An old man and his attorney walked into the office of an IRS agent. The old man asked the IRS agent if he was a betting man, he said yes. So he said I bet you a hundred dollars I can bite my own eye. The agent said you're on. So the guy pulls out a false eye and bits it. The agent was dumbfounded. The old man said I tell you what, I'll bet you double or nothing that I can bite my other eye. Once again, the agent said you're on. So the old man pulls out his false teeth and bit his other eye with it. So now, the agent is pissed because he's down two hundred dollars. So then, the old man said I give you one more chance to win your money back. I'll bet you double or nothing that I can stand on one side of your desk and piss in that trash can on the other side of your desk. The agent looked at the old man and thought there's no way he can do that. So he took the bet. The old man lines up the trash can, pulls out his prick, and started pissing. He didn't come close as he pissed all over the IRS agent's desk. The agent so thrilled by what just happened was smiling and jumping up and down with excitement. Then he looked over at the old man's lawyer whose shoulders were slumped and he had this long look on his face. The agent asked why the long face, and the lawyer answered he bet me a thousand dollars that he could piss on your desk and you'd be happy about it," Mr. Sheridan said with a straight face.

The other guys at the table were laughing themselves silly. Even the guy who brought us over and introduce us could barely contain himself. Then Mr. Sheridan asked looking directly at Denny, "Do you know the moral of the story?"

Denny was shitting bricks. He could barely open his mouth. So I interjected, "Never assume anything."

"That's right, kid! Never assume anything! I don't take money from people I don't know, and if I did, it better be in an envelope!"

"That was a good one Socco!" said the fat man with the baldhead.

I did a double take and looked at Sheridan closely. Could it be? Then I mumbled, "Uncle Socco?"

Sheridan stood up slowly and we locked eyes. Stepping from behind the card table, we began checking each other out from every conceivable angle. "You look familiar. What's your name kid?"

"Neil Wright from New York," I answered.

"Ray's boy! Holy shit!" he pushed an astonished Denny out of the way, and hugged me. Even though I was ecstatic to see a familiar face from the past, his touch and hug still made me cringe. He stepped back and looked me up and down again, "Wow! Little Neil all grown up. I can't believe it!" he remarked hugging me once again. "Where are my manners, let me introduce you to my friends." With a smile as big as Texas, he turned to the brothers at the card table, "Fellas I want you to meet my nephew, Neil. Neil, this is Clarence."

"Nice to meet you," Clarence replied standing up and shaking my hand.

"And this is my right-hand man, Nickel Willie."

Standing up slowly, he cleared his throat several times; tip his hat, before saying, "Hello young man. Nice to meet you, my friends call me Nick."

I smiled and nodded my head. Uncle Socco jumped back in front of me before I could say anything else. "Damn boy, you look just like your daddy! Don't…don't tell me my man Ray is in here too. Ray! Ray!" Uncle Socco yelled, with his head on a swivel looking to see if my father was around.

"No, he's not here. He ah…he passed away years ago."

"Oh my God! I don't believe it! What happened?" he asked ushering me away from the others to talk in private.

"He was murdered when we got mugged right here in Dallas, the night we were supposed to meet you at the train station."

"Shit, I remember that night," Socco replied stroking the top of his head, "I got to the train station a little late, had to run my daughter to the hospital that night. She was running a fever. When I didn't see you or your father, I thought he might have changed his mind or something. I've been looking for him ever since, but nobody heard or knew anything! So where's Estelle? Where have you guys been all this time?"

"I haven't seen my mother since she left us in New York. After my old man passed, I was sent to an orphanage, just got out a couple of weeks ago."

"Hmmm, I don't get that. Estelle loved you guys. You and your father were her life. Something must have happened; she wouldn't just up and leave like that."

"Well, all I know is when I needed her the most, she wasn't there. If she never left, maybe my Pop would still be alive."

"I'm so sorry Neil. I would've come and got you if I knew," he stated patting me on the shoulder. "I will find out who is responsible. And when I do, I promise you they will pay."

"I appreciate that."

"C'mon let's take a walk," he said leading me out the front door. I looked back and managed to catch a quick glimpse of Denny with his jaw on the floor. Still in shock, he just stood there, paralyzed in the same spot with this dumbfounded look on his face.

"You know me and your father go back a long way. I've known him since we were in grade school together at PS 8. We were quite the pair back then. You should've seen us when we turned eighteen in 42' and got our draft cards. Oh, we thought we were big shit. Matter of fact I was there the night he met your mother."

"Really! He never told me.

"Oh yeah, we were on post at Fort Bragg waiting to ship out to Italy. Me and your old man were in an airborne unit, paratroopers," Socco said smiling, "Can you imagine your father jumping out of a perfectly good airplane?"

"No," I said smiling.

"Yeah, well he did. We both did. Crazy huh?

Anyway, we went into town to have drinks in this little pub called…eh…the Blue Oyster. Your mom was in there that night, at the bar, looking so beautiful. Ray was a little shy when it came to the women back then, so he asked me to go over and tell her that he wanted to meet her, and she did of course. I was his best man at their wedding when the war was over. And when you were born, Ray asked me to be your Godfather, and I did. He's like a brother to me, shit he is my brother. We just had different mothers."

"Wow, I didn't know that."

"So you know what that means?"

"No."

"That means we're family too. So, the next time you need someone there, I'll be there. Matter of fact, where are you staying now?" Socco asked.

"With my friend Denny."

"Motor-mouth!" he laughed.

"So you know him?"

"Yeah I know him. Everybody knows him. He never shuts up."

"He's cool; he's been the only one there for me. He's given me a place to stay, clothes to wear."

"Well, not anymore. That's all about to change. Your mother and father might be gone, but you still have family left. Your coming to come stay with us, and I won't take no for an answer."

Subsequently, after going by Denny's and getting my things, Socco drove me back to his house. He actually didn't live that far away, just a couple of streets over. His neighborhood was this long block of large colonial-style homes tuck away just of Forest Avenue, in the heart of South Dallas. You know those classic kind of two-story houses with the big pillars up front holding up a huge covered porch with a swing on it, something that you might see in the movie *Gone With the Wind*. It was painted this turquoise type color with white trim, just beautiful. A quiet area, the residents did a great job of keeping the lawns nicely manicured and the driveways well kept. We pulled into his house and strolled through the front door to hear the sound of a woman's voice yelling, "Socrates Sheridan where have you been! Dinner was served at five o'clock! Your little fast ass daughter already ate and ran!"

"Socrates," I mumbled under my breath trying to fight back my natural urge to giggle.

Sorry I'm late baby," Socco turned and shot me this intense stare, "That name better never leave this house, understood?"

"Yes sir."

Then he smiled at me and playfully punched me in the ribs. I followed him as he walked into the kitchen. Aunt Anita was bent over the sink washing dishes. The dress she had on was a little too short; it exposed her thighs, which looked like she was outside laying face down on a beach chair during a tremendous hailstorm. Socco crept up behind her and gave her a tender kiss on the cheek. "I was held up because I ran into someone this afternoon," Socco playfully said squeezing her around the waist. Her Diana Ross style hair-do hid her face from the side, so all I could see was her coco brown meaty skin.

"Who?"

"Neil," he replied waiving me over. I stepped into her site line and watched her face light up with surprise. Her full lips parted to reveal a mouth full of perfectly straight, pearly white teeth. Denny would be proud.

"Neil, Ray's boy! Oh my God! Come here and give me a hug boy!" She ran over and squeezed me like a pimple, "Look at you all grown up, looking like your daddy. Where are Ray and Estelle, they here too?" she asked almost giddy with excitement as her big, dark-brown eyes scanned me up and down. Socco casually pulled her to the side and whispered in her ear for a moment. It was like magic how the smile was instantly replaced with this somber look. Visibly shaken, she held her composure the best she could as she grabbed a napkin from the counter and dabbed the corners of her eyes before the tears could start to flow. "These onions! They always make my eyes water. You guys have a seat, let me fix you something to eat," she managed to stammer out.

She piled on a mound of food fit for a king. Things I haven't eaten in years, like candy yams, collard greens, cornbread made from scratch, and smothered pork chops with onions. I savored every bite; Anita could cook as good as my momma, which in my eyes was the highest praise you could get.

After we finished eating, Socco took me to their spare bedroom and show me a mahogany chest of draws to put my clothes in. He did everything possible to make me feel at home. So as I began putting my things away and he noticed one of my bags.

"Is that what I think it is?" he inquired pointing at my father's trumpet case.

"Yep, it's my pop's horn."

"You mind if I see it?"

"Sure," I replied handing it to him.

He gently took it from me and looked upon it in amazement shaking his head, "Wow, it still looks the same. Your old man used to love this horn more than life itself. Can you play?"

"Yeah, I still practice often."

Handing it back to me, Socco peeked down

the hallway to make sure the coast was clear. He closed the bedroom door and sat on the edge of the bed and his face turned serious, "So, we didn't talk about this before, but your interest in my crew?"

"Yeah...eh, I really wanted to be part of that family too. That's all we talked about for years in the dorm," I replied.

Socco grinded his teeth for a minute while deep in thought, "You understand the seriousness of this thing you want to belong too?"

"Yes."

"You understand the commitment that will be required of you and the honor and privilege that comes with it?"

"Yes," I said without hesitation. But in reality, I had no clue of the things I'd be asked to do in the future.

Socco mulled it over awhile before rising to his feet. "Ok, I tell you what, I'm going to give you and your friend a chance to prove yourselves worthy."

"Thank you, I won't let you down."

"I know, because I'm going to look after you personally, take you under my wing. Make sure you're around the right element. That's why I'm going to start you off as my driver."

"But I don't know how to drive!"

Socco just chuckled, "Don't worry. I'll show

you." Patting me on the back, he opened the bedroom door, "Feel free to help yourself to anything in the kitchen if you get hungry or something. I'm fixing to turn in, goodnight."

———

Around twelve-thirty, my stomach started growling again. I crept into the kitchen and quietly looked through the refrigerator for something to eat. I found a package of ham and proceed to make me a sandwich when I faintly heard the voice of two girls outside the front door. My curiosity got the best of me, as I walked over to the door to try to make out what they were saying.

"Girl did you hear that same tired ass rap that Gus was trying to lay on me?"

"Heard it! Every girl walking around with a purse has heard that same, lame shit!"

"Hey baby, my name is Gus, and I'm an Aquarius. Anybody tell you, you got the most beautiful eyes. Looking into them is like looking into the future. And you know what I see…me and you together on Saturday night!" both girls said simultaneously, laughing themselves silly.

"Michael was looking cute. I'd hope he was going to say something, but he was acting all scary."

"Because of your daddy! Don't you know who he is?"

"Oh, I know what he is, a *cock-blocker*! That's what he is. Thanks to the great Socco," she mocked with her fingers in quotations, "No man will come within ten feet of me."

"Don't worry about it girl. A real man who's not afraid will step up."

"Yeah, anyway girl, let me get in the house before my momma kills me!"

"Yeah it is late, I'll see you later Foz."

"Bye."

Hearing that, I quickly ran back into the kitchen and continued making my sandwich. The door creaked open and one of the girls tip-toed in the house holding a pair of heels in her left hand, and her purse in the other. She carefully closed the door trying not to make a sound. When she turned around and stepped into the light from the kitchen, our eyes locked for the first time. I immediately recognized the face from my days on the New York playgrounds, but I didn't recognize that body. Oooh we, she was fine. I mean thick like molasses! When Lionel Richie and the Commodores were singing that song *Brick House*, they had to be talking about her! As I gazed into her beautiful light green eyes, I felt myself lost in them. Her full luscious lips opened, and the first thing that came out of her mouth was, "Nigga, who the hell are you!"

I was stunned, and so I stammered trying to

find the right words. She quickly dropped her purse and shoes, reached into her brazier, and pulled out a straight razor. "You better start talking nigga before I slice your ass up!" she commanded moving closer in an attack position.

"Eh, my Uncle Socco said it was cool to help myself to anything in the kitchen," I finally managed to get out.

"Uncle Socco? Who are you?" She asked easing up slightly as her hand holding the blade started to fall to her side.

"It's me, Neil from New York. Uncle Socco asked me to stay here since I just got in town," I replied with my hands up walking slowly from behind the counter, "It's been a long time, but it's good to see you again. It's Fonzie right?"

"My name ain't no damn Fonzie! What you think this is, *Happy Days*! My name is Fozie, Fozie, get it?" she emphasized as she aimed her razor at my neck, "It ain't too late to get your ass sliced up!"

"I'm sorry, Fozie. I meant no disrespect. I actually like your name."

"You do," she asked showing a certain amount of vulnerability for the first time.

"Yeah, it's different, you know …eh… eclectic."

"You really think so?"

"Without a doubt. When people meet you,

hear your name, they'll never forget you, cause you stand out," I answered as I watched Fozie's gorgeous face magically transformed from that mean mug that she flashed me earlier, to a cute child- like simile with these adorable looking dimples. Folding up the straight razor, she tucked it back in her low-cut blouse that barely seemed to keep her large creamy breast from spilling over. I was instantly captivated by them, and I could feel the blood rushing into my dick. I quickly slid back behind the counter to save myself the obvious embarrassment. Plus, I almost forgot just that suddenly, that Fozie is like a cousin to me. I tried to refocus my attention back on the conversation, "So, what made your parents give you such a cool name anyway?"

"I think my father just wanted me to have a unique name like him."

"Well, I wish I had a cool name like that. Neil is so, plain, so average."

"No it's not. I think Neil is kinda cute," Fozie remarked taking a seat on the stool across from me, but never breaking eye contact in the process. Just then, the sound of footsteps that echoed down the hall broke the trance that we were both in. It was Aunt Anita approaching, wearing a housecoat that she clutched at the waist to keep closed.

"What's all the noise out here?" she asked as

her eyes darted back and forth between me and Fozie.

"Nothing, just that nobody told me we had company," Fozie responded.

"If your little fast ass had come home earlier, you would've known. If ya'll are going to be out here talking, please keep it down. I got a long day tomorrow."

Anita went back to bed, and Fozie and I stayed up until the crack of dawn shooting the shit. It was like we were old friends. The familiarity with this family strangely reminded me of home, reminded me of my own family. I hadn't felt like that since I left New York.

J ust like a baby goes from keeping its head up, to crawling, and then walking, so was my maturation process in the *Dark Hand*. Socco schooled me in every way imaginable. First, to be his driver I had to learn how to drive. So he gave me a crash course, throwing me right behind the wheel and on to a busy city street the first day. Second, I had to learn how to dress. T-shirt and blue jeans weren't going to cut it. Socco believed we were professionals, and so we needed to dress the part. So he took me to Reggie's Ready to Wear to buy me a brand-new wardrobe. He showed me the proper way to tie a tie, the difference between straight and French cuff shirts, and Socco even sprung for me my first pair of Stacy Adams shoes. Next, he upped my street IQ and opened my eyes to a world of knowledge I never knew existed. He had me reading books like The Art of War to understand strategies. And with a name like Socrates, you know Socco had me studying not only his work, but other authors and philosophers like Langston Hughes, Oscar Wilde, W.E.B Dubious and Niche.

A typical day for us started around seven in the morning. I'd get up, get dressed, and bring the car around front. Aunt Anita would get up early, around six, and fix Socco the usual breakfast, scramble eggs with cheese, bacon fried crispy, and toast with grape jelly. The highlight of my day was seeing Fozie. I'd sneak a glimpse of her at the table when nobody was looking. Occasionally our eyes would meet, and she'd just start smiling. Her smile was like..... like a beautiful sunrise. It made my day. After that, we'd stop at the corner store to pick up a newspaper, then off to the barbershop for an old fashion shave with a straight-razor, including hot towel treatment. It was one of the ways Socco liked to pamper himself. Next, we made his routine pickups. Socco's main business was gambling. He owned a number of underground sports books and casinos, but he had his hands on a number of other things. Getting kickbacks for rigging construction contracts, prostitution, and offering protection from other gangs to shop owners were just a few of the things that created the vast empire that is the *Dark Hand*. And at each stop that we made, was a nice fat envelope of cash waiting on him. Once all the pickups were done, we'd slide over to Roscoe's Rack Room to hangout, and if there were any additional pressing business matters, Socco was available for counsel. And that's how things rolled for the past few months, until today.

It was a bright sunny afternoon as we headed down Second Avenue on our way to Roscoe's when Socco leaned forward in the back seat and said, "We need to make another stop before going to the office. Clarence is in Houston visiting his mother, and he needs us to make a pickup for him. So stop at that meat market on Oakland."

Clarence was a captain, a leader of a crew. Socco put him in charge of his most lucrative sports book. It was practically a license to print money. If you bet on a game in Dallas, chances are Clarence's crew was taking your action. But the real money came from degenerate gamblers who didn't have enough cash to cover their loses. Clarence and his crew would charge anywhere from five to ten percent vig on the principle compounded weekly. In *layman's terms*, he charged a shit load of interest that you had very little chance of paying off.

"Uncle Socco, you mind if I ask you a question?"

"Sure," he replied unfolding the morning paper.

"This family the *Dark Hand*, how did it start? I mean what gave you the idea?"

I looked in the rearview and saw Socco's eyes staring back at me,

"First of all never say that name in public or mixed company! You never know who might be listening, understood?"

"Yes sir."

"For reasons you will soon learn, this family's business is secret, ok?"

"Yes sir."

"Because of that, I can't tell you too much until you're a member. But I'll give you the basics. Back in New York when I was kid, younger than you, I used to work for this guy named Bumpy. He taught me everything I know. It was his idea for me to come to Dallas in the first place. He wanted to expand our operations, and Dallas was virgin territory. He worked closely with the Italians, even model his organization after them. He saw how for generations the Italians used the structure of a strict chain of command, rules, along with a code of respect and honor to run their families. I brought that same structure here with me and combined it with our culture to form a family and turn a neighborhood that resembled the Wild West, into a peaceful community."

"Hmmm," I mumbled nodding my head.

"Once you prove yourself and become a member, everything will be revealed to you nephew," he said opening back up his newspaper.

As I turned on Forest Avenue, I noticed a black and white police car sitting in the parking lot next to the chicken house. When I passed him, he pulled out behind me and followed us. I was little nervous. His presences had me staring into the rearview mirror. Socco was at ease with his head buried in the morning paper. I turned on Oakland and he turned right behind me. Then his lights came on.

"Socco, behind us," I commented.

He looked up for a moment and continued reading his paper as I pulled over. The cop got out of the car and put on his hat while approaching my side of the vehicle. Hiking up his belt, the hefty looking white man with pale skin and a bushy mustache knocked on my window. I rolled it down and he glanced at me for a second, then he peaked into the backseat, "Well, well, well, what do we have here?" he asked with a smirk on his face, "Let's see some ID kid."

I handed him my learners permit while Socco continued reading his paper. The cop barely glanced at it before tossing it in my lap. He made me get out of the car and patted me down vigorously. Then he turned his attention to Socco, "What about you Mr. Big Shot? What you got for me?" He asked motioning for Socco to lower his window.

Socco neatly folded his paper and sat it in the empty seat next to him. He took his time to roll down his window slowly, "No need to frisk me officer, all I have is this!" Socco said pulling out his thirty-eight revolver, sticking it out the window, and pressing it against the cop's nuts. Both guys started laughing.

"Watch out Socco before you damage the family jewels," the cop joked.

"Don't worry Charlie, I could empty this revolver and not hit anything!" Socco joked as well.

"I heard you had a new driver," the cop commented shaking my hand, "Just busting your balls kid."

"This is my nephew Neil," Socco answered reaching into the breast pocket of his suit coat and retrieving an envelope. He handed it to him, "We good on next Friday night, right? No patrols on Lamar Street."

"Yes sir, no problem," he replied as he looked around to make sure no one saw him stuffing the envelope full of cash in his pocket.

"I love to stay and chat, but we've got to run Charlie. Let's go, Neil."

So I get back in the car and continued driving. I look into the rearview mirror to see Socco staring back at me, "I don't like that pig, but he's necessary for business."

"So you got police working for you too?"

"Everybody works for me."

We pulled up to the meat market on Oakland and I walked around back to open the door, as I customarily do. Socco stepped out and saw this old lady struggling with her bags. He quickly went over and offered assistance, "Ms. Winslow, what are you doing? You know you shouldn't be carrying these bags all alone like this. Here, let me help you."

"Thank you Mr. Sheridan," she replied as her little poodle barked uncontrollably at Socco, "My grandson is at home sick with the flu."

Socco took her bags and placed them in the trunk for her, "Sorry to hear that. Here's a little something to help out." Socco pulled out a money clip full of cash. Peeling off a few dollars, he casually placed it in her hand and gave her a hug, "I hope that grandson of yours gets better soon, and if you need anything, don't hesitate to ask."

"Thank you, you're a blessing," she said getting into her car.

We walked into an empty store; business was a little slow that afternoon. A tall, muscular brother with an attitude came slowly walking up to the front counter, "Can I help you?"

"You sure can," Socco politely responded with a grin, "We're associates of Clarence, the man you placed a bet with. Apparently, you owe him two hundred bucks. We're here to collect."

"Kiss my ass!" The man yelled as he walked from behind the counter, "I'm not paying ya'll shit."

Socco's demeanor never change as he calmly tried to explain, "Look man, you lost fair and square, if you would've won, we'd a paid you your winnings. That's how we do business."

"Fuck you! I ain't paying you shit nigga! Tell Clarence he can bring his black ass in here if he wants, but I ain't giving him shit either!"

"Do you know who I am?" Socco asked politely once again.

"Don't know, don't give damn! You and this punk ass boy don't intimidate me!" he shouted pointing at me as got in Socco's face. He towered over Socco, as Socco only came to his chest.

Smiling, Socco took a step back and threw up his hands in submission, "Sorry for the misunderstanding. We'll get out of your hair, common on Neil."

Socco started to walk to the door, while I could tell that the brother had relaxed a little. Then Socco had turned around and walked back up to the brother still smiling, "I'm sorry man, there was just one more little thing." And Socco kicked the guy in the nuts with everything he had. The brother fell to his knees holding his balls in pain and Socco grabbed him by the throat and hit him with a right cross to the jaw sending him flying to the floor. Grabbing a chair, Socco placed it on top of him pinning his arms down and crushing his throat, barely giving him enough air to breath.

"Now, let's try this again," Socco said as he pulled a switchblade out of his back pocket and pressed the blade against his eye. "You owe Clarence two hundred dollars. I'm here to collect," Socco repeated once again in a polite tone.

The brother coughed and gasped for air as he struggled to speak, "Underneath the register."

"Neil, look under that register over there."

I walked over and looked under it to see a stack of cash crammed under the cashbox. "Looks like about four hundred dollars here Socco."

"Since I've been inconvenience, I think we'll take it all and call it even. What do you say?" Socco asked the brother. The man still pinned down under the chair, looked like he was about to pass out from lack of oxygen, nodded his head in agreement. Socco smiled, got up, place the chair back, and folded up his knife. "You have a nice day buddy. Come on Neil."

※

We went back to Roscoe's where the usual guys were assembling. Nickel Willie, dressed to the nines in a sharp ass suit as usual, was draped over the jukebox looking for a tune to play. Suddenly, he walked in, and when he walked in, he always made a grand entrance. It felt like the place literally shut down and stood still in his presence. A snarky dresser, he wore a lime-green suit with a matching hat that had a long peacock feather sticking out the brim. Black as midnight, his teeth were white as pearls. This flamboyant nigga had the audacity to stand at the front door, open his arms wide like he was expecting a hug, and announced, "Everybody! It's Filmore Locke, the coldest nigga on the block!"

The guys normally got a kick out of it, but I just ignored him and looked for my partner Denny. I saw him and his bloodshot eyes leaning over one of the pool tables. He was holding a cue waiting to take a shot.

"What's happening baby?" Denny yelled loud enough that everyone's head turned. Sitting down his cue, he pulled me to the side, "Give me skin blood! Shit, I ain't seen you a minute."

"Me and Socco was just handling the normal business," I responded as I gave him a dorm 6 handshake, "What about you? How's everything going with Locke?"

"Eh, he's got me being an errand boy! Getting his coffee and picking up his dry cleaning, you know menial bullshit! No real action blood."

"I guess you just gotta be patient. These guys are all about paying your dues," I reasoned. "By the way, I got a letter from Frito."

"Oh yeah, and what did big boy have to say?"

"He's going to be out by Thanksgiving, and

Mousey by Christmas. I can't wait. We're going to have our crew, one big family man!" I said almost giddy with excitement. I missed my boy, especially Frito. Denny was not as enthusiastic.

"That's cool," he uttered with a forced smile, "But what about this errand boy shit? I need some bread baby."

"Just be cool, I got a feeling things will fall into place soon," I added when I felt a hand touch me on the back of the shoulder. I turned around to see a beady-eyed Locke flashing his pearly white teeth at me.

"Neil, Socco's favorite. What's happening slick?" he asked. I hated anyone touching me, but something about Locke really made my skin crawl.

"Hey Locke," I replied doing my best to be cordial.

"You gotta come down to Harry Hines and get at me sometime. I got a new stable of bitches that are finer than cat hair. Any itch you got, they'll sure enough scratch it."

"Thanks I'll keep that in mind."

Locke turned toward Denny rubbing his belly with his massive hands that were covered with gold rings. "I'm starving! Say slick, slide on over to Catfish Lloyd's and pick me up a three-piece tails, fried hard and some fries. And make sure you get hot sauce with it this time," he commanded slapping Denny on the back, "Catch you later Neil."

Denny gritted his teeth, "See what I'm talking about."

"Just be cool man."

Socco came strolling back over and broke up our conversation, "Neil, something has come up. We need to make another stop. Hey Locke," he said as he whisked me off without two words for Denny. I took another quick glimpse back before we darted out the door to see the look of frustration on Denny's face as he rubbed his red nose.

We pulled into the parking lot of the barbershop I went to when I first got out. The lights were still on, but the place looked empty. As Socco and I approached the front door, he stopped me and locked eyes with me, "I just got a call before we came from the family of my friend Veronica. Apparently, this guy in here, Henry, has been abusing her. She's in the hospital now for a cracked rib and a broken jaw. Her mouth has to be wired shut. Veronica is a good friend of mines, so this is personal to me. I want you to send this bastard a message for me."

"What kind of message?"

"That there are consequences for hitting women."

"What do want me to do Uncle Socco?"

"Remember what you told me about your

father? Remember what you told about the guy that picked on you in that orphanage?"

"Yes."

"Well, it was a guy just like him that did it. Go in there and show him that good people like you don't deserve that. Release your fury," he urged as he opened the door of the barbershop for me.

I walked in to see that all the chairs were empty. Then this brother comes walking out the back whistling, cleaning his hair clippers. I instantly remembered his face. He was one of the guys talking about me when I was trying to find Denny for the first time. Socco's words began to resonate, and my blood started to boil. I couldn't even see his face anymore, all I could see was Mark and lazy eye. My eyes scanned the room, and a metal mop handle caught my attention. I casually walked over to it, and started unscrewing it from the rest of the wet mop. The guy looked up and saw Socco standing in front of the door with his hands in his pocket, "Mr. Sheridan, hey, can I help you with something? You need a trim?" Henry asked.

"So you like to hit on women?" Socco asked in a patronizing tone.

Henry's eyes grew wider as he now noticed me holding the metal handle. "I don't know what you're talking about."

"Veronica's mother called me and told me

what happened. Did you know that she is about to get her jaw wired shut thanks to you," Socco added, inching closer. I inched closer as well on Henry's flank.

"Mr. Sheridan, with all due respect, this is a private family matter between me and my wife."

"You made it a public matter when you decided to hit her," Socco replied.

Henry was speechless after that. His mouth was moving, but no words came out. I just continued to get closer and closer while he looked around searching for a way out. I gripped the handle tighter. With each passing second my anger grew, the emotions I had inside came rushing out. I could literally feel Mark on my back, penetrating me again. It was like I relived that nightmare all over again. I reared back like baseball player who just found the right pitch, and I swung away. Oddly enough, the sound of the metal handle striking his shoulder blade was similar to that of a bat hitting a baseball. I stood over him and took another ferocious swing, and another, and another, and another. Bruised and bloody, Henry cried out in pain. Finally, Socco grabbed me as I beat Henry within an inch of his life.

"That's enough," Socco ordered, "Message sent."

His touch snapped me back to reality. For a moment, it was Mark that I was hitting. I slowly dropped the handle, took a deep breath, and followed Socco out of the door. He took the keys from me and decided he'd drive himself. It was a quiet trip on the way home. Neither one of us said a word. When we pulled into the driveway, Socco killed the engine and turned to me.

"Neil, you showed me something tonight. I liked the way you handled yourself and how you followed orders. That's good, real good. Look here, I got an opportunity coming up very soon for you to make your *bones*. Everything goes right; you'll become a member."

"Really," I replied. I was so excited I could barely contain myself. Those were the words I'd been waiting to hear since I got out.

"Yes, just be ready."

66 ood morning Socco," I said with great enthusiasm taking my seat at the breakfast table. I was about to move into my first place today. Socco and Aunt Anita were cool for giving me a place to stay, but I was ready for my own pad. I had stacked my bread ever since I first started working for Socco. He was paying me four hundred dollars a week, which was a nice hefty sum for a youngster like me. And with no expenses, I already bought my first ride, an old Mustang. Now all I needed was my own apartment. Plus, I wanted to be set up for when Frito gets out next month.

"Morning Neil," Socco replied buttering some toast.

Aunt Anita was putting the last of the food on the table. Sitting down next to Socco, she planted a kiss on his cheek. Fozie came strutting out her bedroom wearing this black leather mini-skirt and a cute blouse showing off her mid-drift. She sat down next to me and crossed her sexy legs.

"Mommy, daddy," Fozie acknowledged, and then she looked at me batting her eyes while smiling, "Good morning Neil. So are you excited about moving?"

"Bitter sweet, I'm excited about getting my own apartment, but I'm going to miss you guys."

"Well you're family Neil, so you're always welcomed here," Aunt Anita added.

"Daddy, I'm going to help Neil decorate his new place, I need some money," Fozie interjected.

"Oh, and don't forget I need some cash too baby. I got to go grocery shopping to get the stuff I need for the church's bake sale this weekend," Aunt Anita added as well.

Socco pulled out his gold money clip stuffed with cash. He peeled off a few dollars, and handed the cash to Fozie and Anita.

"Thank you daddy," Fozie responded in her soft little-girl voice, which was as phony as a three dollar bill, before kissing him on the cheek.

We spent that afternoon shopping for pictures, furniture, and other knick-knacks. Fozie had a great eye for decorating. She dragged me down aisle after aisle mixing and matching the right centerpiece for the coffee table I bought, or pictures that accentuate the champagne colored couch I had delivered the day before. It seemed like we hit every shop on Buckner Ave, before heading to my new place. I got a flat in East Dallas off Samuel Blvd in Clarence's territory. The property manager, Vince, got in to Clarence for five large, so he rented me the apartment for next to nothing as part of his debt to Clarence.

"You got a really nice place Neil. Once we have everything situated, I think it'll be cute," Fozie commented as I opened the door and we sat the last of the bags down.

"Thanks, so have you thought about moving out and getting your own place?" I asked pouring us something to drink as Fozie stood in the middle of the room, staring at the walls, looking to see how she wanted to position the furniture.

"Well, I was staying at the dorm in my freshman year, but after the summer, I started thinking *what's the point*? The college is not that far away. The allowance my daddy gives me goes further at home with no expenses. Plus, I think I like to be married when I officially move out," she added with this sinister looking grin.

"Really," I replied blushing. "So what's your major anyway, I don't think I ever asked?"

"I don't know yet. I'm just taking the basic courses now. Socco says I should take accounting. I think he just wants someone he can trust counting his loot."

I nodded my head acknowledging what she just said while strolling over to the turntable and thumbed through the few albums I owned, "How about some music?"

"Sure," she replied carefully centering a picture over the couch.

I finally found my favorite Earth Wind and Fire record. It was a little scratched up from me playing it so much, so I put a nickel on top of the needle to keep it from skipping.

"Oh yeah, I can dig that groove!" Fozie said bobbing her head to the beat while singing, "You're a shining star, no matter who you are, shining bright to see, who you can truly be."

I began singing along with her as we started doing *the bump* and grooving to the music. We continued singing and moving while I grabbed the hammer and nails and started nailing up the pictures as she positioned them. I was hammering the last picture and now *Sing a Song* was playing, and Fozie was still dancing with her back to me. She had on her customarily mini-skirt with some sexy looking go-go boots and a cashmere sweater. The conversation my eyes were having with her ass caused me to lose focus. So much so, that I missed the nail and hit my thumb.

"Ouch!" I yelled out dropping the hammer.

"What's wrong?" she asked quickly turning around.

"I hit my damn hand."

"Let me see." She softly, gently, took my hand

and carefully caressed it. Then the song changed once again, and now the sultry slow jam Reasons was on. We gazed into each other's eyes, and it was as if there was nobody else in the world but us. I moved closer, ever so slightly, and so did she. It was the first time, since my father died, that I actually felt at ease, comfortable with someone touching me. Our lips were only inches apart, then... a knock at the door.

"I guess I better get that," I said slowly tearing myself away from her tender grip. I opened the door to see Denny standing on the other side.

"What's happening baby?" he exclaimed barging through the door and playfully jabbing me in the ribs. It had become common by this time that his eyes were always bloodshot, and his nose was swollen and red as a stoplight.

"Hey."

"I just came by to check out your new place, looks nice," Denny added looking around. "Hi," he said smiling at Fozie. She was clearly annoyed and forced a grin while heading to the bathroom.

"Say, is that Fozie, Socco's daughter?"

"Yeah."

"What the hell are you doing having her up in here alone?"

"She's helping me decorate."

"I bet she is!" he remarked sarcastically as he sniffled in between every word, "You playing with fire blood. If Socco finds out you've been getting fresh with his little girl, he's gonna put something long and hard inside of you, and it ain't gonna be dick!"

"He wouldn't do anything like that. Socco considers me family, right?" I said scratching the back of my head trying to convince myself as well as Denny.

"That shit doesn't matter if he knows you fucking his daughter! He'll snatch your damn nuts off and use them for dice nigga!"

"Maybe you're right. Where are you heading anyway?"

"I'm going over to Locke's and give him a piece of this score I landed last night. Meet me at Roscoe's when you get finished here."

"Sure, you okay man? You look a little strange," I noticed.

Denny rubbed and squeezed his nose and put on some shades to hide his red eyes, "I'm fine baby, cool as a cucumber."

Denny took off right about the time Fozie came strolling out of the bathroom. Looking at her face, it was apparent that she'd been working on her makeup in there. Her lashes, lipstick and eye shadow was touched up. She walked over and sat next to me on the couch.

"Why do you hang out with Denny?" she asked holding my hand and scooting up underneath me.

"He's my friend."

"Be careful about the people you call friends."

"Why?

"Losers can bring you down if you're not careful."

"You think Denny is a loser?"

"If the shoe fits."

"You just don't know him like I do. He's cool people," I reassured her.

"Well I overheard my daddy saying that he has something big lined up for you. That if things go right, you'll be on your way to become a part of the family," Fozie added, as her soft little hand gently began to caress my chest. Her touch continued down a path that included my stomach, around my waist, down my thigh, and finally stopped at my knee. I could feel the beat of my heart quicken in the process. My palms were sweaty as I could feel my dick getting harder and harder.

"You know I love your scent," she whispered in my ear.

"Really?"

"Oh yeah," she replied moving even closer, to where her supple breasts were pressed against my arm. Her hand began to glide back up my thigh and was only inches away from my dick. I had never been with a woman before, but my natural, primal, animalistic instincts were beginning to kick in. I wanted to take her in my arms, suck on her neck, rip off all her clothes, and thrust my body on to hers. But that's when Denny's words began to resonate, and all I could think of was the possibility that Uncle Socco could walk in any moment and catch us. The thought of it made me recoil and hop up off the couch.

"You okay?" Fozie asked.

"Yeah, yeah," I stammered, "I'm fine. Denny just reminded me of an appointment I had. I gotta be there in thirty minutes. I better go ahead and take you home." I said nervous as hell. Denny's words had hit home, and I wasn't about to be killed over a girl.

With that, I took Fozie back home and cruised on over to Roscoe's. Denny's words were resonating in my head the whole trip over. It's undeniable the way she made me feel, but now I was seriously concerned how Socco would react. He treated me like family, opened his home to me, and helped me get on my feet. He gave my life direction and purpose; I certainly didn't want to do anything to disappoint him. It was a lot to think about.

I walked in to see Nickel Willie standing by the cigarette machine. He just bought a pack of camels and was peeling off the wrapper, "Hey, I was hoping to run into you, and here you are, Johnny on the spot."

"Hi Nick."

"I needed to talk to you. Why don't we take a stroll," he asked removing a handkerchief from his breast pocket, and coughing into it vigorously. He wiped his mouth clean, lit up a square, and opened the door for me to follow. Nickel Willie moved quite well for a man his age that used a cane.

"So, are you ready to *make your bones*?"

His question took me totally by surprise. I knew this day was coming. I just didn't think it was coming this soon. "Yes," I mumbled.

"I just got the order that someone has got to go," he said taking a drag of that square.

"Who?"

"Denny."

"Denny! Are you sure?" I asked completely puzzled.

"Look here kid, you're a soldier. Orders come down from the top. You follow them. No questions asked. That's how this thing is done," Nickel Willie stated rather coldly.

"But...but...Denny, he's my friend! He's cool. It's got to be a mistake. Let me talk to Socco and straighten this out."

Nickel Willie dropped his cigarette on the curb and stomped it out. Turning toward me, his eyes, which were cold as ice and black as midnight, started to burn a hole right threw me.

"There are no buts. No mistakes. The decision has been made, and it's final. If you want to be a part of this family, you'll have to learn to do what you're told. "

I let out a deep sigh. Seeing my frustration, he looked into the blue sky in deep though for a second and showed me a little humility for the first time. "You're a good kid, so I'm going to break my own rule this one time and break this down for you. You wanna know why your friend got the axe, fine. Denny is a fucking punk! He's a loser and an embarrassment to this family. The boy is selling and using drugs, breaking Socco's number one rule. And you're being asked because Denny trusts you. You can get close to him without raising suspicions. And Socco is giving you an opportunity to prove yourself."

"I understand," I mumbled once again. It started to dawn on me. His weird behavior, his need for more money, the bloodshot eyes, was all signs that Denny was out of control. It was a tough pill to swallow. I liked Denny, and considered him a friend, but if he violated a rule like that, and broke the code, dishonored the family, then he deserved whatever fate Socco deemed necessary.

As we approached the bus stop, Nickel Willie took a seat on the bench and clutched his cane with both hands. He began to cough violently again before he eventually cleared his throat, pulled out another cigarette, and started smoking again. "Tomorrow night you're going to ask Denny to accompany us out to White Rock Lake. Tell him we got a big score lined up. I got a special gun you're going to use, completely untraceable. We're going to get him comfortable, show him a little product. I'll give you a signal, a tug on the lapel on my jacket. That's when you tap him, two to the head, understood."

"Yes sir."

"Good boy. Don't worry, this will be easy."

I nodded in agreement, but down inside; I was conflicted. Although Denny was a loose cannon, he was still my friend. And despite what Nickel Willie said, nothing about killing my friend was going to be easy to me.

Reluctantly, I did as I was told. I convinced Denny to go with Nickel Willie and me out to White Rock Lake that Friday night. It didn't take much convincing to get Denny to go. Once I told him it was a big score involving Nick, he was in. All he saw was the dollar signs, an opportunity to move up and make a name for himself.

We pulled up to his place about six in the evening. Since it was fall, the sun had already set, and the streetlights were on. Denny came out dressed to impress. He had this very nice white turtleneck sweater on, a new pair of freshly pressed brown corduroys, and a black leather coat. Rhonda stopped him at the door, whispered something in his ear, and gave him a kiss goodbye.

"Hey Neil," she yelled turning toward me and waiving.

I waved back as Denny eagerly raced down the stairs and opened the rear door of Nickel Willie's sky blue Fleetwood Cadillac. I turned around to shake his hand as he climbed into the backseat, and of course, he gave me a dorm 6 handshake. And for that moment, my mind wandered back in time and remembered all the things we went through, the fun times we had together.

"Gentlemen," Denny said seemingly on his best behavior. I looked into his eyes and was surprised to see that he was sober, a rarity.

Nickel Willie's demeanor was as cool as a cucumber as he turned and smiled at Denny. Almost like he was a proud father taking his kids on a nice leisurely drive to the country. We sped off into the night.

Arriving at White Rock Lake about twenty minutes later, Nickel found a spot in an isolated parking lot next to a wooded area. The area was well lit from a combination of street lamps and a full moon that filled the clear sky that night. The smell of charcoal and barbecue sauce filled the air as I could see the publicly used grills and picnic tables that surrounded the lake. Denny and I followed Nick to the back of the car as he searched for the keys to open the trunk.

"Check this out boys," Nickel Willie said as he pulled out a box cutter and opened one of several boxes that were neatly packed in his trunk. Pulling out a gold watch, he handed it to Denny, "Top of the line quality."

"This is nice merchandise," Denny observed before handing it on to me.

"Yeah I got a guy from California that can score this stuff for me. He only charges me twenty-five a piece, but I can get at least seventy-five from places we control around here. But I got too much on my plate right now, so I'm a turn this over to you boys," Nick stated closing the trunk.

"Really," Denny added. I could see the dollar signs in his eyes.

"Yeah, he likes to meet me out here, out of sight. He doesn't like anyone knowing who he is. But I have a good relationship with him. I've earned his trust. So he'll do business with you. Come on, I'll introduce you," Nick said leading the way down this cemented trail that led into the wooded area. Denny and I followed closely behind as the car started disappearing from sight. After a few minutes, our hiking ended as we arrived at a small clearing that was in the middle of nowhere.

Denny walked out in front of Nick and me, looked around, and asked, "So where is this guy?"

Nick turned toward me and tugged on the lapel of his trench coat. I reached into my waistband and pulled out the Saturday night special that Nick had given me earlier. My hands were shaking violently. I aimed it at the back of Denny's head, but I couldn't pull the trigger. I froze. That's when Denny turned back around.

He saw the gun pointed at his head, and was immediately alarmed.

"Neil, what are you doing? Why are you pointing that piece at me?"

"Shoot him kid!" Nick commanded.

"Wait a minute! There's got to be some misunderstanding! Let me talk to Mr. Sheridan. We can clear this right up," Denny pleaded.

"Shoot him kid!" Nick urged once again.

"Please don't kill me!" Denny begged falling to his knees, "I'm sorry for whatever happened! Please, Neil, don't do it! We're friends!"

I stared into Denny's pleading eyes with the gun still pointed at his face. It would have to be the one time when they weren't bloodshot red. A gust of wind was blowing through Denny's perfectly cut afro, as he put his hands together like he was praying for a miracle. Nick was creeping closer, reaching for the forty-five, he kept in the small of his back, just in case I didn't have the nerve to finish the job, I'm guessing. Suddenly, my nerves finally calmed down and my hands stopped shaking.

"Please Neil, my friend, don't kill me," he pleaded one last time.

"Sorry Denny," I said as I took a step forward and squeezed the trigger. The shot hit him in the neck and he fell backwards holding his throat. I moved closer and stood over him. The blood was squirting out as Denny struggled to breathe. His legs were violently twitching. His eyes were wide open staring at me. It was as if they spoke to me, like how the hell could you do this to me when I brought you in. They gave me pause, but only for a second. I placed the barrel of the gun against his forehead and squeezed off another round.

"Damn kid, you had my worried for a minute. You okay?" Nickel Willie asked taking off his hat and wiping his brow with a monogrammed handkerchief.

"No," I replied continuing to stare at Denny in shock. Half of his brains were decorating the ground beneath him, a gruesome site. I got an instant headache as I rubbed my ears, they were still ringing from the loud sound of the gun blast.

"The first time is always the toughest, but you did well kid. Now, go ahead and drop the gun."

"You sure?"

"Yeah, just drop it next to him, it's untrace-able. Don't worry," Nick reassured me.

In a trance, I let the Saturday night special I used slide out of my hand. It landed next to Denny's lifeless body. Nick put back on his hat and used his cane to make his way over to me. Coughing fiercely, he wiped his mouth with the handkerchief, lit up a cigarette, and took a real long drag off it. He patted me on the shoulder and then made his way back down the path. I followed him into the car, and then Nick reached into the crease of his seats and pulled out a flask.

"Want a drink whiskey?" he offered.

"No."

"You sure, it'll take some of the edge off?"

"My mother was an alcoholic. I saw how it destroyed her and tore up my family. I'll never touch the stuff," I replied shaking my head.

"Suit yourself kid," Nick said taking a big swig.

"How do you deal with...you know?"

"It's a job kid, like flipping burgers, or washing windows. I don't! I do the job asked of me. I go home, feed my family, and sleep well. I don't think about it afterwards. I've seen so many people die, that I'm numb to it now anyway."

"But how did you get that way. It doesn't bother you. You think about God, or the ten commandments, or any of that stuff?"

Nickel Willie took another long swig, "From the time I was old enough to walk, I was in church. Thursday prayer service, Tuesday Bible study, the sermon on Sunday morning, seemed like I was in church every day of the week. We were dirt poor, so I prayed for money, but God never answered. The Klan threatened my father, so I prayed for his safety, God never answered and they lynched him. My older brother got tuberculosis. I prayed to God that he'd heal him,

God never answered; he died in a sanitarium when he was twenty. After all the things I've seen in my life, I'm convinced. God doesn't give a damn. He plays favorites with a few, and says the hell with the rest us."

Nickel Willie's words really hit home. I remembered the countless times that I was on my knees praying that my mother would come get me, praying that my pop wouldn't die, praying that I wouldn't get raped, and he never answered. Nick was right!

CHAPTER 20
NOVEMBER 12 2011
MATHEW WRIGHT

Sister Simmons was speechless. The old lady's legs were like spaghetti, and she almost lost her balance after hearing my father's story, "My God! I need to sit down," she said placing her Bible on the foot my father's bed. She grabbed some Kleenex from the stand and wiped the tears forming in the corners of her eyes.

"I told you," my father said taking another drink of water. "I don't think I slept for a week after that. Every time I closed my eyes, all I could see is Denny's face right before I shot him. It took a while to get over that, but I eventually did. Nick was right; it was just a job, nothing more, nothing less. If an order comes down to punch a guy's ticket, so be it. I do it and not think twice about it."

"You can't possibly believe that God doesn't care?"

"I've seen no evidence to the contrary," the old man replied grimacing, clinching the sheets. The pain medication had almost completely wore off.

"God allows things to happen to you for a

reason; to humble you, to bring you closer to him, to trust him."

"Hmmm."

"Dare I ask what happened next?" she said regaining her composure.

"Well, my career went to the next level after that. I made my bones, and a couple of months later, I was made an official member of the *Dark Hand*. I shouldn't tell you this; if I had found out that anyone talked, I'd have them killed. But being I'm dying anyway, what the hell. They had a ceremony for me in the basement of the civic center that Socco donated to. I was ordered to be dressed in a black suit with a red tie. Socco, Nick and all the captains, Clarence, Locke, James, and Lee were dressed just like me, stood side by side in front of this long card table. On the table was this brass collection plate, a lighter, a needle, and a picture of Jesus. Socco took my left hand and pricked it with the needle. Then he said, "Blood is required to join, and the only way out is by blood." He held my hand over the plate and allowed my blood to drip inside of it. Then he squeezed my hand and asked me to raise my right hand and repeat after him. "I swear to put this family first, before all others, including my children, my wife, and God. I swear to follow the orders of the boss at all times. I swear to follow all the rules of this family, to be available whenever I'm needed. I swear to keep all family business secrets from all outsiders." Then he picked up the picture, lit it with the lighter, dropped in the collection plate, and said, "A man's word means everything. May your soul burn in hell like this picture if you break your word in any way." Socco and the rest of them walked from around the table and embraced me like a brother. It was one of the proudest moments of my life. I belonged to a family again. It was like I achieved my purpose in life, that I found my place in this world. I fulfilled my destiny, and was becoming what I was born to," my father said smiling.

Shocked, Sister Simmons sat up in her seat, "Unbelievable!"

"Yeah, that's right about that time that things really begin to get complicated. Frito finally got out, and the fellows decided to throw me a surprise birthday party, a sort of welcome to the club type party. Funny thing about parties though, there's always an unexpected guest. But even I didn't know that this bastard was going to show up and crash the party."

CHAPTER 21

FEBRUARY 5 1975
NEIL WRIGHT

S occo had me to pick him up for some business he needed to take care off. So I swooped by his place around nine o'clock that night. Nobody did anything special for me that day. No gifts or anything. But it didn't bother me though, I was used to it. All the years that I spent in that home, I never got a gift, a card, nothing but smiles and happy birthdays from my buddies. Anyway, I rang the doorbell and Fozie was there to greet me.

"Hi Neil, happy birthday" she said greeting me with a big hug and a flirtatious smile. Once again, she was looking so fine in these skin-tight blue jeans and a gray halter-top that had her creamy breast just oozing out of the top. I found myself helplessly staring at them again. I squeezed her waist and held her close to my heart. My natural instinct was to kiss her as we backed up and our eyes locked. And those eyes, damn. I get lost in them every time I see her. They were so magnificent and inviting. I think she used them to entice me whenever I gazed into them. But just then, Aunt Anita walked up behind her and snapped me back to reality.

"Happy birthday Neil," she said also.

"Thanks."

Fozie grabbed my hand and led me into the living room and on to the couch. "There's something special I wanted to do for you for your birthday."

"What?"

"Let's go to New Orleans for Mardi Gras. We can hangout for a week, have fun with all the celebrations on Fat Tuesday."

"New Orleans for a week, I don't know," I replied scratching my head. All I could think about was her and me alone, in a hotel room, at night, with nothing standing between me and her fine ass body but a thin camisole. Damn!

"C'mon, it'll be fun. Besides, Socco won't let me go if you don't come. He doesn't trust anybody going out of town with his little girl, but you," she asked with pleading eyes laying her cute face against my shoulder.

I sat there mulling it over for a minute, "Ok," I finally answered.

"Thank you, thank you!" she yelled hugging me.

Socco came walking out the back dressed in a clean, Italian cut, double-breasted, gray suit.He grabbed his keys off the kitchen counter while adjusting his tie and said, "I see Foz convinced you to take her to New Orleans?"

"Yeah, I've heard about it before, it should be fun."

"I'll set you guys up with a couple of real nice rooms, right in French Quarter."

"Thanks."

"You just make sure nothing happens to my little girl," he said slapping me on the back while walking past me toward the front door, "Now let's go before we're late."

We arrived at a hotel suite, when Socco gave me the key to the door, asked me to open it, and took a step back. As soon as I opened the door, a room full of people yelled surprise. The entire *Dark Hand* family was there, including my boy Frito, who was just an associate and not yet a member. I was elated, like a child on Christmas morning as I walked in. Nobody, besides my parents, went out of their way to make me feel so special. The suite was spacious with vaulted ceilings, a living room, dining room, a fully stocked wet bar, and a kitchen all nicely furnished. On the top floor over looking downtown, the view was breathtaking. Every guy in the family came over and showed me love, and embraced me like a brother. A waitress with a tray of champagne glasses came out the kitchen to offer one to everybody. Socco grabbed two, and handed one to me. He took a fork and banged it against the glass to get everyone's attention.

"Hold it down for second, I want to make a toast," he announced. The room fell quiet. Socco lifted his glass and stated, "To Neil, our newest brother. You are now, and forever surrounded by family my nephew. Cheers."

"Cheers!" everybody yelled tossing back their drinks. I raised mine for a second, before sitting it down without taking a sip. Socco leaned over and said to me, "You okay?"

"I'm fine. I just don't drink. Not after what I saw my mother go through," I replied.

"Well, I'll drink for the both of us," he added as he finished his drink, and then killed mine as well.

The door opened to the bedroom and out walked Locke in a peach colored three-piece suit with the hat to match. With his chest poked out, and his legs cocked opened like he had a ten-pound dick between them, he announced, "It's Filmore Locke, the coldest nigga on the block. And I got an extra special treat, bitches so fine; they'll knock a nigga right off his feet," Locke proclaimed as he pointed to a DJ who was set up in the corner, "Maestro if you please!"

The DJ started playing *Brick House* by the Commodores as a group of ladies wearing nothing but bras and panties came strolling out the bedroom single file. Locke was many things, annoying would be at the top of my list, but one thing he isn't, is a liar. Every woman was super fine! The guys were whistling, yelling, and groping the ladies as they taunted the men by dancing erotically. While I was enjoying the show, my attention was diverted by a knock at the front door. Since I was standing the closest to it, I opened it. I immediately recognized the face! I'd seen the face in my nightmares for year. It was the face of the man who stole my life. It was that black bastard, lazy eye!

"Guess who's here?" he yelled at the top of his lungs.

Socco heard the voice and turned around, "Ronnie! When you get out?" he asked grinning, giving him a hug. The rest of the guys, upon seeing this son of a bitch, were jovial as they came running over.

"I just got out this morning boss!" he replied enthusiastically, "After two long ass years in the pen, all I want is a decent meal and some pussy."

"Well, I think we have both buddy. By the way, I want you to meet my nephew, and our newest brother, Neil," Socco introduced me.

I was speechless, stunned. I had no idea what to do. Lazy eye, Ronnie, or whatever the fuck his name was had his hand extended waiting for me to shake it. I was so overcome with emotion that I just stood there. Socco and Ronnie looked at each other oddly, and then Ronnie came over and hugged me!

"I know this can all be overwhelming my friend. You'll get used to it. Welcome to the family brother," he told me.

He walked off, grabbed a woman, and started conversation with her on one of the couches. Before I even had a chance to digest what just happened, I felt an arm slide around my shoulder.

"If it ain't the man of the hour!" Locke said, "Look here slick, I got something extra special just for you." He led me to the bedroom and opened the door. Lying across the bed wearing a teddy was this beautiful woman who was the splitting image of Jayne Kennedy.

"Neil, meet Belinda the blinder," he said grinning ear to ear. Leaning over, he whispered in my ear, "Baddest bitch in my stable. They call her the blinder because she's guaranteed to make you gush out a vanilla shake, if you know what I mean." He joked elbowing me in the ribs. Shoving me into to the room, he winked at me and said, "She's all yours, enjoy slick."

She sat up in the bed on all fours and crawled over to the edge. Her eyes were mysterious as they surveyed me. Looking me up and down while her lips curled into a devilish smile. Grabbing my hand, she pulled me closer to the bed, "Come over here and relax, I won't bite sugar."

I obeyed her commands, not really knowing what I was doing. My mind was racing with all kinds of thoughts, and none of them had anything to do with her. I wanted to go back down stairs, get the thirty-two snub nose pistol I just bought, and put a bullet in the head of that lazy eye bastard Ronnie. The feeling of anger began to overtake me to the point that I didn't realize that Belinda had unbuckled my belt, slid down my zipper, and was slowly peeling off pants like a ripe banana. She massaged my back, as her fingers rippled down my spine like she was playing a piano. Then she slowly pushed down my briefs.

"Nice," she commented, and then her lips kissed the head of my dick. That sensation sent shockwaves throughout my body. It jolted me back into reality and I grabbed my pants and pulled them up quickly.

"Stop!" I yelled backing up.

"It's okay. You don't have to worry about catching nothing. I'm clean sugar," she responded moving closer again. She tried touching me again.

"Don't touch me!" I yelled again.

"What's your problem? What, I'm not good enough for you?" she asked hopping to her feet and putting her shirt back on.

"Just leave me the alone!" I snapped jerking the door open. I was still a virgin, and the whole idea of having sex with her just didn't feel right to me. She came chasing after me, and the commotion caught the attention of everyone in the suite. The party turned to a full-blown orgy at that point. Frito, with his pants around his ankles, had one of those chicks bent over a chair nailing her from behind. Locke was lying on the couch with one woman riding his dick, and another sitting on his face. Ronnie had another chick on the kitchen counter with her legs wrapped around his waist going to town. Even Socco was in on the act getting his jimmy waxed in an armchair.

I tried fastening my belt and straightening my clothes, but Belinda wouldn't stop harassing me as I tried making my way to the front door.

"What's your problem? What…you a queer or something?" she yelled. Before she could get out another word, I wrapped both hands around her neck and tried to wring it like a wet dishrag.

"Whoa, whoa!" Locke yelled running over to break us up, "What's going on?"

"This crazy bitch won't leave me alone!" I responded still choking her. Frito ran over and helped Locke to pry her neck from my grip. They finally managed to separate us after a fierce struggle on my part. Belinda fell to the floor gasping for breath. Locke was stunned, as he knelt down to check on her.

"What happened?" Frito asked.

I didn't answer. I was still so angry. I turned and tried to walk away. Locke popped up and put his hand on my chest to keep me from leaving, "You owe me some answers. You damn near killed her."

"Get your damn hands off!" I yelled pushing him away. Locke went stumbling backward.

"You little motherfucker!" Locke yelled trying to regain his balance.

"Hey, Hey," Socco loudly interjected stepping between me and Locke. "Everybody just calm the fuck down!"

"You better get this kid Socco. I don't know what his problem is. First, he damn near strangled one of my girls to death, and then he gets fresh with me. He needs to be taught some manners," Locke added.

Socco, who managed to get dressed first, snatched me by the arm and ushered me outside the room and down to the lobby. It was late, so the only person down there was a front desk clerk doing some paperwork.

"What the hell was that?" Socco barked pacing back and forth.

"That black, lazy eye guy that just got out of prison."

"Ronnie! What about him?"

"He ah…"

"He what? Spit it out!"

"He's the one that killed my father," I finally stammered out wearing this stoic look.

Socco's eyes got wider than a silver dollar, "You positive?"

"I could never forget a face! NEVER! That man killed my father!" I said moving closer and locking eyes with him.

Socco continued pacing back and forth scratching the back of his head, "I know you want revenge."

"Revenge! Revenge would be going to his folk's house, killing his mother, father, brother, sister. Going to his house and if he has a wife, killing her and his kids. Then I'd have revenge. Then he'd be just like me with no family left. That would be revenge. That would make us even. I'm not asking for that. I'm asking for an eye for an eye, his life for my father's life."

"I believe you Neil. I do. Look, I loved Ray; he's like a brother to me. I want to see Ronnie answer for what he did to him too. But you can't just go up there and whack him. He's a member, a connected man with lots of friends. You go after him, his people will come after you and this family will have a civil war on its hands. Just be patient nephew," Socco pleaded staring me in the eyes. He put his hands on my shoulders and massaged them in an attempt to calm me down, "I promised you that the man responsible for killing your father would pay, and he will. But you have to let me handle it, and set it up right. Trust me, okay?"

I let out a deep sigh before eventually nodding my head yes in agreement.

"Good, nobody knows about this, and we need to keep it that way for the time being. Now, I want you to go back upstairs and apologize to Locke for what happened."

"What! Apologize, to that bastard?" I barked, annoyed once again.

"A bastard he might be, but he's also a captain, and you were out of line talking to him like that. That's how this thing works. And I'm going to have to tax you for putting your hands on him, a thousand dollars."

"Damn, c'mon Socco," I said punching the wall.

"You can't put your hands on another member. How's it going to look if I let you slide? The rules apply to everybody Neil."

I begrudgingly went back up stairs, shook hands, and apologized to Locke. That was the easy part, but it took everything in me not to rip that lazy eye bastard apart. I stayed cool and kept my hands off Ronnie, for the time being, anyway. I trusted Socco to do right by me, so I'd wait.

Things smoothed out over the next couple of weeks. I became Socco's official enforcer under Clarence and his crew. So if I did a hit, like the one on Denny, I'd get five grand. If I had to rough a guy up for non payment on a loan, gambling debt, etc., I'd get twenty percent of whatever I collected. I was expected to kick up to Clarence ten percent of whatever I made. The captains, in turned, kicked the same percent up to Socco. A monetary system Socco referred to as "tribute" for using his name, connections, and police protection to operate. It worked beautifully, like a well-oiled machine.

With everything falling into place at home, Fozie and I headed to New Orleans and Mardi Gras for our vacation. Socco was true to his word. He got us two first class airplane tickets and a two-bedroom suite in the French Quarter. The scene there was crazy. Being from New York, I'm used to seeing crowed streets and people walking around in weird clothes, but New Orleans was different. There was so much debris floating in the air from the people standing on the balconies above. I never seen so many people drunk out of their minds before. Women were doing anything for some beads, included flashing their tits and riding around on guy's shoulders twirling their shirts in the air. I even had ladies I didn't know, just walk up, and French kissed me. It was wild.

Fozie was getting into the act too, drinking tequila shots until she was slurring her words, and could barely stand up. She was constantly falling all over me, hugging my neck, and playfully rubbing my chest every time we took a few steps. Her flirting was tough to handle because she was looking so fine as usual. Even though it was chilly outside, that didn't stop her from wearing her customary halter-top, leather mini-skirt, and pumps. It was funny how guys were breaking their necks to check her out. Back home, that would've never happened, brothers were too scared of Socco. Out here though, guys were practically undressing her with their eyes.

Our first night there we went to eat at this famous Cajun restaurant around the corner from our hotel. After waiting a half hour for our table, we finally sat down to eat. As the waiter took our menus, I caught this slick hair, white guy staring at me from across the room. I paid it no mind at first, until this well dressed man got up from his table and walked over.

"Excuse me, sorry to interrupt, but your name Neil?"

"Yeah," I replied trying to make out his face.

"It's me, Pete!" he said smiling.

"Pete! What's happening, my man," I said jumping to my feet, and bear hugging my friend until he started to turn blue, "Damn boy you changed. You got this new sophisticated looking going down! I like it. Looks like you're doing well."

"Thanks man, but I'm not doing as well as you," he responded looking at Fozie, "Who is this beautiful woman who you're with?"

"Oh this is just my friend Fozie. We flew in from Dallas for Mardi Gras."

Fozie cut her eyes at me for that, guess she didn't care for the fact that I introduce her as just a friend. She stood up and smiled at Pete though. Pete took her hand and kissed her wrist.

"It's a pleasure to meet you Fozie. If all the women in Dallas are as gorgeous as you, I must get up there for a visit," Pete added.

Fozie blushed, as he she flashed her girlish smile that I found so irresistible, "Thank you, nice to meet you too Pete," she replied turning toward me, "I like this white boy Neil."

"You mind if I have a moment alone with Neil?" he asked.

"Sure, I need to powder my nose anyway,"

Fozie replied grabbing her purse and heading toward the restroom.

Pete watched her leave then grabbed her chair and took a seat, "So did Frito hook up with you when he got out?"

"Yeah, he's staying with me, working with me. He's doing fine."

"What about that Denny, and the whole *Dark Hand* thing he used to go on and on about."

"He got me in there, introduce me around. Turns out my long-lost uncle was the boss. I started out being his driver, now I made my bones, and I just became an official member of the family."

"Really, congratulations brother. You know I've been out here doing the same thing, working for my uncle."

"So how's that going?"

"I've been trying to work my way up the food chain. The old man has me running the pier."

"The pier?"

"Yeah, we control the piers, docks, and everything else near the shoreline. We can get our hands on damn near anything you can imagine, cigarettes, whiskey, guns, hell even little kids bikes. Only problem we have sometimes is that New Orleans is small, and we don't always have enough clientele."

The wheels in my head began to spin. We

controlled the black-owned business in Dallas, and had major influence over many others. I thought about it for a minute, and then I had a brilliant idea, "I might be able to do a little business with you Pete. You know we have many businesses that we associate with, and Dallas is a fast-growing city. I think we can strongly influence them to take those kinds of items, if the price was right."

Pete smiled and nodded, "I think we can definitely do business my friend. Matter of fact, I got some prime stock I'll be getting my hands on over the next couple of weeks. What you got going on in the morning?"

"Nothing, probably just sleeping in."

"Anybody I deal with has to be okayed by my uncle. I'm supposed to be meeting with him in the morning, why don't you go with me?"

"Okay," I responded. Pete pulled a pen out of his pocket and jotted down where I was staying just as Fozie was making her way back to the table.

"Great, I'll pick you up in the morning. You guys enjoy the rest of your evening," Pete said with subtle waive making his way back to his table.

After dinner, we went club hopping until

about two in the morning before going back to the hotel room completely exhausted. Fozie was still buzzing a bit, and I never touched a drop of alcohol. Fozie stumbled into the bathroom, while I went into my room, shut the door, and stripped down to my boxers.

"Goodnight," I said while cracking the door. With eyes heavy, I slipped under the covers. Ever since the *Mark incident,* I always slept on my back, and now it's become a force of habit.

I could hear a door shut and saw the lights in the hallway go out from the crack under the door. The place became quiet, and my eyes feel close as I drifted off. Being an extremely light sleeper, I was awoken a few minutes later by the slow turn of my doorknob. The door crept open, and I heard the faint sound of footsteps across the floor. Fozie, now dressed in nothing but an over-size t-shirt, climbed on the bed and straddled me. Her body was pleasantly warm and soft. Leaning forward, she whispered, "You've been running from me a long time, but I got your ass now."

"Fozie please, we can't do this," I responded trying to sit up a little.

"Neil, I always get what I want, and I want you."

"But what about Socco? He'll kill me!"

"Forget about him! What about me? Don't you want me?" she asked stripping off the t-shirt, and

Goddamn! She was fine, everything I could've ever imagined, and more. I could tell she had just oiled down her sexy, voluptuous figure. My mouth watered as I admired her sumptuous breast and perky nipples. I quickly forgot about Socco and everything else.

"Yes I want you. I always wanted you, but I have never done this before."

Fozie put her hand over my mouth and said, "Leave it to momma." She pulled back the sheets and climbed under the covers with me. She snuggled up to me tightly and gave me the sweetest, longest, and most passionate kiss I have ever known in my life. It was the first time, since my father passed, that a touch was pleasing. She buried her face in the middle of my chest and took a big whiff, "I love your scent," she said softly in my ear.

"You do?"

"Yes, and guess what else?"

"What?"

She sat back up and looked me eye to eye, "I love you, Neil Wright."

The words caught me off guard, but they were welcomed. Before I even knew what happened, the words were flying out my mouth, "I love you too."

Fozie's hand probed under the covers, searching for my hardened dick. Scared, I tensed up and scooted back in the bed. She gave chase, scooting up with me, kissing me softly on the neck, "It's okay baby. I won't hurt you," she whispered in a soothing voice. Her little hands found what she was looking for, as she gently grabbed my dick and massaged it. Rubbing my chest to put me at ease, she let out a subtle moan before mounting me and placing me inside her warm wet pussy. It was exhilarating, a magical sensation, almost as if our bodies were made for one another. I started to loosen up, as my hands got a mind of their own. They gently stroked her soft thighs and caressed her curvy hips, pulling her closer to me, as I penetrated deeper and deeper. She slowly began to ride me, as she put her hands on my chest, and twirled her hips in a grinding motion. I was quickly getting the hang of this, matching her rhythm stroke for stroke, as the thrust quicken, and our breathing got heavier. She wrapped her arms around my neck, kissing me all over my face while I squeezed her waist as tightly as I could. I felt like a teakettle about to whistle after the water finally reached its boiling point. The intensity came to a peak as the thrusting got faster and faster until my body seized up and I exploded inside of her with all the passion that had built up in me. The most thrilling five minutes I ever had. What can I say, it was my first time, shit!

That next morning while Fozie still slept, I went down stairs and waited for Pete to pick me up for our meet. He took me to this social club called the Corner. When we entered, I immediately felt out of place. The club was filled with nothing but Italians and every one of their eyes was suddenly focused directly on me. They had a look on their face like how does this nigga have the audacity to come in our place. Pete led me into the backroom where two grey-haired, well-dressed, Italian men, were sitting at a table sipping coffee. One of the men looked at me, placed his coffee cup back on the matching saucer, and quickly exited with his head down. The other man, whose hardened face looked like it had been chiseled out of stone, cut his cold dark eyes at me, and asked Pete, "Who is this person that you bought in my place?"

"This is my friend Neil I was telling you about," Pete responded with a stoic face as he tried to introduce me, "Neil, this is my uncle, Victor Marcello."

I extended my hand for him to shake, but he just looked at it, picked up his coffee, and took another sip.

"I don't do business with niggas. Pete should know better," he replied

"But Uncle Vic we grew up together. Neil is like a brother to me. He was there when nobody else was. I owe him."

I stepped in front of Pete and cleared my throat, "Mr. Marcello, we grew up in a terrible, violent place. To survive we had to form our own brotherhood, where loyalty, honor, and a man's word meant everything, because it was all that we had. Those are the relationships that I hold sacred to this day, and aren't relationships necessary when doing business sir?"

"Yes they are," Victor replied taking another sip of coffee, then sucking his teeth. There was a long uncomfortable silence. He stared at me for a moment, and then back at Pete. Finally, he slowly rose to his feet and looked deep into my eyes, almost as if he was searching for something. "Okay, if Pete is vouching for you, you must be a stand up guy. But I don't know your organization, so if I do business with you, I do business with you exclusively. Nobody else is to know of our arrangement, understood?"

"Understood, you have my word," I said as Victor finally shook my hand. I smiled as I made my first deal. All I could think about was the endless possibilities to make money.

More than a year went by and I continued to grow. No, I don't mean in height or physical stature, but in cash and power. I had no idea how lucrative my business connection was going to be with Pete. I became the number one earner in the whole family giving Clarence a fat envelope with at least five grand a week in it. I had so much cash; I didn't know what to do with it. So I just put it into a shoebox until the shoebox got full, and then I stashed it in my closet. Last check, I had over a couple dozen shoeboxes.

I needed help to run the operation, so I formed my own crew. Mousey was now out and all too eager to put in work and make a name for himself, and Frito, who had come into his own after he replaced me as Socco's driver for the past year was ready to make some bread. We'd meet Pete half way between Dallas and New Orleans in a little small town right on the border called Shreveport. I'd hop into the truck and drive it back to a South Dallas warehouse with Mousey and Frito fully strapped in the car behind me, just in case someone tried to hijack me. My first shipments were whiskey. Most liquor stores in Dallas were all too eager to buy their supplies from me. I was saving them twenty-five percent off wholesale cost from the distributors they normally used. The few that resisted got a little visit from Mousey and Frito. After being harassed constantly, having their windows busted out, and their deliveries disrupted, they eventually fell in line.

I made a pawnshop my base of operation where I kept an office in back to do business out of. I didn't really know anything about that sort of business, but thanks to a bet, I became a silent partner. I was sitting at my desk that morning when a casually dressed Socco unexpectedly came strolling in one late afternoon.

"Hello Neil," Socco said taking a seat in one of the armchairs. It was his first time checking out my office. He looked around at the walls and admired the pictures of Thelonious Monk, Charlie Parker, Miles Davis, and John Coltrane. "I like the way you decorated."

"Thanks."

"I didn't catch you at a bad time, did I?"

"Of course not."

"Good," he replied reaching into the pocket of his button down shirt and fishing out two cigars, "Want one?"

I was stunned because I had never seen Socco offer anyone a cigar before. I contemplated for a second because I never drank or smoked, but I modeled myself after Socco. I tried to dress like him, handle business like him. So when it came to a cigar, I thought *what the hell.* "Sure," I replied taking one from him and holding it against my mouth waiting for him to light it. I took a drag off it and started coughing. Socco came over and patted me on the back.

"Easy, don't inhale it, just taste it in your mouth. Enjoy the taste and aroma," he added smiling. After I cleared my throat and wiped my eyes, I did as he said. Socco was right. It didn't taste half bad.

"As you know, I've had my eye on you, and I'm impressed how fast you've come along and how you've become a top earner. You handle business well. You seem to be a natural," Socco commented.

"Thanks."

"This operation you got going is pretty big. You've been moving a lot of product.

How you come by it?"

"I like to tell you Uncle Socco, but my connection wants to remain anonymous and I gave him my word," I responded shrugging my shoulders.

Socco just smiled as he rose to his feet, "I see. Well, I got two pieces of good news for you. I'm promoting you to captain."

"What," I said in shock.

"I'm putting you in charge of your own crew. I'm making Frito and Mousey official members, and you can decide on who else you want to add. You'll be dealing directly with me and Nickel Willie now."

"Wow! But why?"

Socco took another puff off his cigar and slid his arm around my shoulder. "I'm getting old nephew; you're the future. You're a natural leader, and I'm going to start grooming you to be my successor. Soon you'll be my number two, and I'll be giving my orders through you and you only. Eventually, you'll take over as boss."

"But, but what about Nickel Willie?"

"Nick is an old man. His time is short. Clarence, Locke, those other guys, they're soldiers, earners, but not leaders. You're the future my friend."

"I'm honored. Thanks Uncle Socco."

"Congratulations," he said giving me a bear hug.

"So what's the other thing you were going to tell me?"

"Oh yeah, I have another surprise waiting on you in the car. A very special gift," Socco said smiling heading for the back door. I followed him outside to the parking lot, and over to his car. Sitting in the driver seat was Ronnie. Ronnie saw me, smiled, and nodded. I looked at Socco feeling confused.

"I don't get it. What's that lazy eye bastard doing here?"

"You've waited patiently for a long time. I know how hard it's been, and I appreciate that. But now, you don't have to wait any longer. It's time you honored your father. He's all yours Neil."

I stared at Socco in admiration. He already had my respect and loyalty, but with that act, I was ready to follow that man anywhere, even into the bowels of hell! I checked the waistband in the small of my back to make sure that my thirty-eight revolver was still tucked in. I eagerly hopped into the passenger seat next to Ronnie. Socco climbed into the backseat and ordered and unsuspecting Ronnie to drive us to a meat packing plant in East Dallas.

We arrived at sunset and Ronnie jumped out of the car first to open the door for Socco. Socco took one last puff off his cigar before tossing it to the curb. "Come on and let's get this money this guy owes me. I don't wanna be here any longer than absolutely necessary," Socco commanded playing along. Socco led the way across the large parking lot just as the streetlights popped on with me and Ronnie side by side following closely behind.

"So Ronnie, me and you rarely get a chance to rap."

"I know," he answered shaking his head, "Been really busy since I got out, trying to get on my feet."

"Yeah I know how that can be. So have you always lived in Dallas?"

"Yep, born and raised. What about you?"

"I'm from New York City."

"Oh, okay, just like Socco right," he added smiling.

"Are your folks from here too?"

"Yeah they still live in the same old small house off Hatcher for the past thirty years. What about you? Your kinfolks still live in New York?"

"Naw, I haven't seen my mother since I was twelve, and my old man was killed when I first moved to Dallas."

"Really? Damn, that's fuck up! What happened man?" Ronnie asked as we followed Socco through these large double doors and into the long steal corridor. Socco came to a stop once the doors closed behind us and turned around.

"We got robbed downtown near the train station by these two guys after we got finished eating at this little diner back in 69. One of the guys got into a tussle with my father, and stabbed him to death. Funny, one of the guys was named Ronnie just like you. He even looked like you,"

I said as I reached into my waistband and pulled out my piece, cocking the hammer.

Ronnie turned and faced me, looking me up and down with that lazy eye, "I think you got me confused with someone else buddy."

"Naw I don't think so. I could never forget the face of the man that took my father's life. I could never forget the face of man that put a knife to my throat and threaten to kill me."

"What the hell is going on here Socco?" Ronnie asked as his eyes darted back and forth between Socco and me.

"The wages of sin is death, time to pay up," Socco responded with a stoic look.

With vengeance in my heart, I pointed my pistol at his kneecap and took a shot. Ronnie screamed out in pain as he fell to the ground holding his knee. He scooted away from me and propped himself against the wall.

"How does that feel, you asshole?" I asked sarcastically.

"I knew I should've cut your throat when I had the chance," Ronnie retorted, defiantly.

Pissed off at that response, I shot him again in his other knee. He screamed again as he wallowed around on the floor in pain. I squatted down to one knee, "Got anything else to say?"

"Fuck you punk," he yelled still defiant to the end.

"You right handed Ronnie?"

"What if I am?"

"I just wanted to know what hand the knife was in when you stabbed my father," I replied as I shot him in the hand. Cradling his hand, he curled up in a fetal position in pain. Walking over, I shot him again, this time in the gut for maximum pain, and because it'll take longer for him to bleed out. And I wanted to savor every moment of his suffering. "That was for my father, you bastard!" I shouted as I stood back up and put the gun back in my waistband. Socco and I leaned against the wall for the next twenty minutes and watched as Ronnie took his last breath. And I have to be honest. I enjoyed every moment.

"Alright grab his feet so we can take him in here and cut him up," Socco commanded, "We have to Amelia Earhart this guy."

"Amelia Earhart?"

"Did you guys study any history at all while you were in that orphanage?" he asked shaking his head as we carried Ronnie's corpse into the next room, "She was the famous lady aviator who disappeared while flying cross country. We are going to make Ronnie disappear, just like her. He has too many friends, and he's too well connected. So if anybody asks, he left town with some broad, understood?"

"You're the boss," I said nodding my head.

We brought the body into a huge freezer that had slabs of meat hanging from large hooks. Stripping him of his clothes and tossing them into a garbage bag, we put the body on this large table saw the meat packers used to slice the beef into roast, steaks, etc. Socco fired up the saw and began cutting off each of his limbs and head. We bagged the remains, made sure that the coast was clear, and tossed the bags in Socco's trunk. Socco looked at his watch.

"It's only nine; Earlene's doesn't close for another hour. Why don't we slide over there and get us some oxtails and black-eyed peas. I'm starving?"

"Sure."

On the drive over there, I can remember having a nice feeling of satisfaction. Lazy eye finally paid for what he did to my old man. All seemed right with the world, now that he wasn't in it. After we grabbed a bite to eat, he dropped me off at the pawnshop and dumped the body in White Rock Lake. We never talked about this incident again.

———⬥———

When I got home that evening, Fozie was there waiting on me as usual. We had been seeing each other secretly over the past year, ever since that trip to New Orleans. Fozie was clever she'd sneak over, tell her momma she was staying at friends, something like that. I even gave her a key. She'd come over, clean up my place, and have a hot meal waiting for me when I got home. That night when I walked in, she was sitting on the couch wearing one of my dress shirts, which I found so sexy.

"Hey baby," she said springing from the sofa to rush over and give me a kiss, "How was your day?"

"Great! Your father gave me a promotion," I said putting my keys on the table. After spending so much time together, I could look at Fozie's face and tell something was on her mind, "You okay?"

"I got something I have to tell you," she replied twiddling her thumbs.

I walked over to the sofa, took off my shoes, and had a seat. "Lay it on me baby."

"I went to the doctor last week because I've been sick lately, and my period is late. He ran some test, and the results came back today," she said sitting on the couch holding my hand.

I sat up on the edge of the couch, "What is it?"

"I'm pregnant."

My first thoughts were *Socco is going to kill me.* Then I thought about I'm actually going to be a father, wow. I had a mixture of feelings. My mind was scattered in several directions, and I couldn't find the words to tell Fozie how I felt. The only thing I could do was force a smile and give her a hug.

"Neil I have to tell my father."

"I don't know Foz."

"Well we'll have to do something soon. I'll be showing in a month or two," she said as she lifted her shirt and showed me her stomach. I gently rubbed her belly and kissed her navel. Fozie flashed me that youthful schoolgirl smile, "You know what I was thinking?"

"What?"

"I was thinking that if we got married, Socco would have no choice but to accept us as a couple."

"I couldn't marry you without Socco's blessing. It's only right. Besides, we deserve a big wedding with all our friends and family there."

"So does that mean you want to marry me?" Fozie asked wrapping her arms around me and burying her head in my chest.

"If you can promise me you won't have that hell damage on your legs like your mama," I joked.

Fozie laughed, "Very funny. You better love me no matter what!"

"You know I will baby," I said kissing her on the forehead, "Of course I want to marry you baby. I love you more than anything, and I look forward to spending the rest of my life with you. I don't know how long that life will be once Socco finds out though."

"Don't worry, I'll tell my mother first. She'll be mad, but she'll be supportive when she finds out. And we can let her break the news to Socco."

"That's cool, but I have to talk to Socco, man to man. Tell him that we've been seeing each other, and ask for his blessing to marry you."

Fozie was so elated that she jumped into my arms and wrapped her legs around my waist. I fell backwards on the armchair as her luscious lips planted kisses all over my face and neck. She started ripping my clothes off like a woman possessed, throwing my shoes and pants across the room.

"I want you now!" she commanded, not bothering to take off her own shirt. She just climbed on top of me and started riding. Holding me tightly, she grinded like she never grinded before. I thought we might break the chair the way we bounced up and down, slamming it into the wall. She grabbed the arms of the chair for leverage, and leaned back allowing me maximum penetration. The way she bit her bottom lip with every stroke, the way she tilted her head back and I could see the sweat trickle down her neck and into her cleavage, the way she moaned and screamed "Oh daddy!" when a brother went deep in, just turned me on. I tore that pussy up that night. Damn!

The next day was normal, routine, despite the fact I had a lot on my mind. I woke around eight, got dressed, and visited my father's grave. It was a place of solitude, where I could go and reflect. Spending time with my father always put me at peace, helped me to think clearly. I'd always bring fresh flowers and clean his new headstone that I got him after I started making a few dollars. Sometimes when I'm in a sentimental mood, I would bring his trumpet and play some of his favorite songs. I continued to take lessons twice a week over the years. I had improved immensely since the days when pop forced me to practice my scales in New York. After I got finished there, I stopped by Shirley's Donuts for a bear claw, a cup of coffee, and the morning paper. And just like my mentor Uncle Socco always instructed, I never sat with my back facing the door. Being a member of the *Dark Hand* is far different from being a civilian. We have to have our heads on a swivel and be prepared at all times, because you never know what could jump off. Next, I slid over to my office at the pawnshop to hold court. That's when

Mousey and Frito came strolling in. Both guys impeccably dressed as normal. Frito was wearing his favorite colors, a navy blue shirt, black slacks, and he loved wearing Italian shoes with the tassels so that he didn't have to worry about tying up his shoes. And Mousey was sporting a grey suit with a red button-down shirt. It was an unwritten rule that Socco wanted us dressed professional when we're out conducting business and representing the family. I noticed that Mousey walked in bow-legged and grimacing.

"What's wrong with you," I asked Mousey who gingerly sat down in one of the armchairs across from me.

"This dumb bitch gave me the clap," he snapped massaging his dick, "I've been pissing razor blades all week! Shit!"

"You haven't seen a doctor yet," I inquired.

"Yeah, I just got back. I got to take this damn penicillin for the rest of the week," he replied showing me his prescription bottle.

"What happened? Who gave it to you?"

Frito was busting a gut as he plopped down in the other chair and kicked his feet up, "Remember that chick Sandy that we warned Mousey not to fuck with?"

"Sandy?" I asked.

"Yeah, you know the one that got those sharp teeth like she's been chewing rocks!"

"Oh, you talking about Dracula!" I replied cracking up with Frito, "I hope you didn't let her put those fangs on your dick?" I asked. Frito's infectious laugh had me in tears.

"Very fucking funny!" Mousey snapped again.

"Grrrrrr," Frito growled flashing his teeth and pretending to take a bite at Mousey's dick.

"Stop playing!" Mousey shouted pushing Frito away.

"Okay that's enough. Let him be Frito. I really can't joke myself because I got woman issues too," I said.

"With who? We never even seen you with a chick," Frito said.

"We've been seeing each other secretly for the past year."

"And you've been keeping this from your boys! Who is it?"

"I'll tell you, but you guys can't say a word to nobody, understood."

"Scout's honor nigga, now spit it out," Mousey responded sitting on the edge of his seat.

"I've been seeing Fozie."

"Socco's daughter?" Frito asked.

"Yeah."

Mousey and Frito stared at each other in amazement, and then back at me. "Damn!" they both yelled out.

"That's not it. She's pregnant."

"Socco is going to kill you man!" Mousey blurted out.

"No he's not, he thinks of him as family," Frito added, "What are you guys going to do?"

"We're going to have the baby and get married."

"That's a good idea! You marry her and he might not kill you," Mousey added.

"I'm not going to marry her to appease Socco. I'm going to marry her cause I love her, and it's the right thing to do. I always wanted a family of my own. We all did. That's all we ever talked about growing up."

"So you're definitely going to tell him?" Frito asked.

"Yeah, when I check in at Roscoe's this evening."

"Good luck," Frito said shaking his head.

"Oh, I got some good news for you guys. I talked to Socco yesterday; he's making me a captain and giving you two memberships. We're going to be an official crew!" I announced enthusiastically.

"I don't believe it!" they said as we all shared hugs and dorm 6 handshakes with each other. Just then there was a knock on the door and Jimmy, the guy who I'm partners with and who runs the pawnshop, poked his fat head in through the cracked door, "Hey Neil, Andy is here."

"Send him back."

Andy Carmichael, a shrewd white council-man from the twelfth district, came in my office smiling, shaking all of our hands, "Afternoon gentlemen."

"What's shaken Andy?" I said reaching into my desk drawer and pulling out a envelope with about fifteen hundred dollars cash in it.

"About to hit the campaign trail my friend. I got a fundraiser this evening. The primary is in two months," he responded with a goofy looking smile while rocking back and forth.

"I always like to help out a civil servant," I said casually passing him the envelope, "By the way; I'm going to need you to speak with your friends downtown about several more liquor licenses and tax permits I need. I got a list right here," I said as I handed it to him.

He took the paper from me, opened it, and scanned over the list, "No problem Neil. Well, I got to run. Tell your uncle I said hello."

———

I was on edge that evening when I checked in at Roscoe's like normal. The usual suspects were there, but I noticed none of them as I paced back and forth twiddling my thumbs and rubbing the back of my neck raw trying to figure out the best way to tell Socco about Fozie and me. I walked over to the jukebox nervously tapping my fingers against the glass searching for a song that would calm my nerves. Socco walked up behind me.

"Neil you okay? You don't seem yourself," he asked before taking a puff off his cigar.

"I need to talk to you about something important."

"Ok, why don't we step outside?"

We stepped outside on a cool, damp, overcast night. I couldn't take it anymore, so I cleared my throat and just blurted it out, "Uncle Socco, Fozie and me have been seeing each other for a while."

"Really," he replied stoned face, staring at me and taking another puff off his cigar, "And?"

"And, uh, I love her, and she loves me."

"And?"

"And, uh, I want your permission to marry her."

Socco, still stoned face, stared at me long and hard before tossing his cigar aside, "So you've been seeing my baby girl behind my back?" he asked coldly.

"Yes sir, I didn't mean to. I guess we were just drawn to each other."

Socco slowly stepped closer to me, "I only have one thing to say to that!" he snapped balling up a fist and raring back like he was getting ready to hit me, "Welcome to the family boy!" he joked giving me a massive bear hug.

"You're not mad?"

"Of course not! I know you two have been seeing each other."

"You have?"

"Boy, I could tell the way you were looking at my daughter when you met her, and the silly looking grins every time you were around each other, that ya'll have something going on."

We both laughed. I felt like a tremendous weight had been lifted off my shoulders. I breathed a sigh of relief as Socco put his hands on my shoulders, "Look here Neil, I always thought of you as the son I never had. I could never take the place of your father, but I love you just the same, and I couldn't think of a better man that I would want my daughter to marry. You have my blessing."

He embraced me again and kissed me on the cheek. I could feel the tears forming in my eyes. His continuing approval, love, and support meant everything to me. With Fozie on the other side of town smoothing things over with her mother, everything was right again.

That fall, Socco threw us a big, beautiful wedding. It was outdoors in October, which can be risky in Dallas, but everything turned out wonderfully. It was the social event of the year. A variable who's who from the Dallas social scene was on hand to witness the nuptials. All of Socco's friends from politicians to sports figures showed up, not only to see and be seen, but to show Socco respect. Of course, all my friends from the underworld were there too. Nickel Willie and all the captains, including that bastard Locke, showed up to the affair. Frito was my best man, and I think he was more nervous than I was, because he dropped the ring during the ceremony. Socco proudly walked his daughter down the aisle and gave her away. But the most special thing about that day was Fozie. She was so beautiful, and she had a glow about her that just brighten the room when she walked in. Now eight months pregnant, she looked like she could pop any day, dressed in a gorgeous white gown that was so long, she needed four girls to walk behind her and hold her train.

The only thing that could rival that day was my son being born a month later. We welcomed Mathew Raymond Wright into the world November 3, 1976. At eight pounds seven ounces, he was everything I dreamed my son would be and more. A handsome little baby, he looked liked my father. He had his eyes. Frito and Mousey agreed to be his Godfathers at the christening a couple of weeks later.

As for my other family, business couldn't be any better. With Frito and Mousey members, and me as the captain, we were an unstoppable team. Our operation was like a virus. It just grew and grew. I had connections in Fort Worth, San Antonio, and Houston by this time. When I first started getting shipments from Pete, I got a load once a month. Now, I was getting them every week, sometimes twice a week. And the inventory, anything you could imagine. Guns, alcohol, cigarettes, purses, televisions, refrigerators, anything Pete's guys could get their hands on. We had a massive pipeline of stock going all over the state. I went from giving Socco two thousand dollars a week tribute, to almost twenty thousand dollars. I easily became the biggest, most powerful, and best earner of all of Socco's captains. Remember when I said I put shoeboxes stuffed with cash in my closet. Well, after a couple of years of the money rolling in like it did, I had so many shoeboxes in my closet that I barely close the door anymore. I couldn't even believe it until Fozie and I actually counted all the cash. I was a fucking millionaire!

The first thing that Fozie suggested we do with the money was buy a house. So I bought a new four-bedroom house, uptown where all the white folks were. I spared no expense fixing the place up. Everything was top of the line. We were the first in our neighborhood with a remote controlled television and a microwave. The next thing I spent major cash on was my wardrobe. I took it to another level. I hired the best tailor in Dallas, and had all my suits custom made with the finest of fabrics, like Egyptian cotton. Next, I bought us new cars, a Cadillac for Fozie, and a Mercedes for me. And last but not least, I took Fozie and my newborn son on a first class trip back to New York City. We stayed at the Ritz Carlton, ate at Sparks Steakhouse, and shopped at Neiman's Marcus. We were on top of the world! Little did I know that world that I spent so much time carefully constructing over the years was about to be turned upside down, and all my friends and family's loyalties were about to be tested.

I got up that morning around seven as usual.

While I got dressed, Fozie was in the kitchen whipping up breakfast. I also got my son dressed and we were in the kitchen just about the time Fozie was putting our plates on the table. I placed little Mathew in his highchair and shared my plate of bacon, grits, and biscuits with him. As I cracked opened the morning paper and took a sip of coffee, Charlie was ringing the doorbell promptly at seven-thirty. Charlie, a neighborhood kid who worked himself up through the ranks, became my driver a year ago. A tough little bastard, he knew how to handle a shotgun before he was old enough to grow hair on his little nuts. His attention to detail, willingness to do what the next man won't, and most importantly the fact that he grew up with Nickel Willie's grandson Jacob, had him one step away from becoming an official member.

"Good morning Mrs. Wright," Charlie said with a big smile as Fozie opened the door and let him in. The super tall Charlie had to duck under the entryway to keep from hitting his head.

"I told you to call me Fozie," she responded, "You hungry, want something to eat?"

"No ma'am."

"Negro please. I can hear your stomach growling over here. Sit down. I'm gonna fix you a plate, and I'm not taking no for an answer," Fozie commanded as she already fixed him a plate and sat it on the table. He wolfed down breakfast while I finished reading my paper. As we got ready to leave, I kissed Mathew and Fozie on the cheek before darting out of the door.

"Oh baby, remember to pick up our dry-cleaning," Fozie reminded me.

"Okay Foz."

Charlie sprinted over to my car and opened the door for me. It was weird at first, being waited on hand and foot, but it was something I got used to very quickly. I pulled out a cigar. Ever since Socco gave me one, I've been addicted to them. The moment I stuck it in my mouth, Charlie was prepared to light it. We hit the streets to make my rounds, but I had Charlie stop at the dry-cleaners first.

I walked into the store; it may have been about four or five people standing in line. When the owner saw me come in, he stopped what he was doing and ran a got me my clothes first, "Hello Mr. Wright, I have your things right here. I took care of these personally," he said walking over and shaking my hand vigorously.

I reached in my pocket and pulled out my money clip to pay for it, when he stopped me, "Your money is no good here Mr. Wright. Have a nice day, and tell your wife I said hello."

"Thank you sir. If you ever need anything, let me know."

He smiled and shook my hand again while the people in line looked on in amazement. We got back in the car and continued to make my rounds. Every stop had a fat envelope full of cash waiting on me when I arrived. And just like the dry-cleaner, I never waited. After we finished, I stopped by Roscoe's.

When we pulled up, I saw Nick out front as usual, sitting on a stool, giving away change to all the neighborhood kids who wanted some. I strolled inside to see the same cast of characters decorating the place. Only thing that was different was that Clarence finally had the jukebox updated a few months back. So now, I can actually shoot a game of pool to music that's not thirty years old. Socco and Locke were sitting at the furthest table in the back drinking and talking when I walked up.

"Socco, Locke, what's shaking fellas?" I asked reaching into the breast pocket of my suit to fetch my weekly envelope. I casually passed it to Socco, "It's been a good week."

"I see," Socco commented smirking while squeezing the envelope before slipping it into his pocket.

"What's happening slick?" Locke added shaking my hand. The tension between us is still there, but not quite as bad as before.

"I'm good," I replied trying to be cordial.

"Walk with me," Socco said opening up the back door to the alley. We stepped outside on a warm afternoon. The sun was shining brightly on Socco's face, so I followed him over to the shaded side of the building. "I got an old friend of mine that's coming in from New York next week. He's looking for some special stuff, and if we can get it, he can promise us something real big. Only one problem, he only trusts me and wants to deal with me. I was thinking maybe it's time you introduce me to your friend and arrange a sit down. This way, I can broker this deal. It could be worth millions!"

"I talked to him recently on my last run, and he's just as adamant as he's always been about keeping his identity secret. I wish I could I tell you who he is, but I gave him my word, sorry. Maybe you could introduce him to me. I am quite charming. He could warm up to me."

"Yeah right," Socco sighed, "We'll see."

I started to walk back into the bar when Socco said, "Hey, there's one more thing. Jesse has to go. Locke is going to take care of the problem tonight. I want you and Frito to go along with him. Make sure this gets taken care of properly."

"What happened?"

"Locke found out he was dealing coke. You know the rule. Deal and die."

"I understand. It will be done."

—◁᠁◁◐᠁▷—

So later that evening Frito and I met up with Locke and Jesse at a nightclub in far East Dallas called the Raven. It was a little hole in the wall strip club that Locke owned and ran his business out the back of. I didn't like it at all. The situation was strange to begin with. Socco never asked me to do a hit with Locke before. My crew had always worked alone. Socco would give me the name of a guy who needed to be taken care of and I would make sure that it was carried out to a tee. Like this asshole name Maury. Through Socco's contacts, he found out that he was a snitch. Socco wanted to make an example of this bastard. That's when he called me. I slit his throat, cut his tongue out, stuck it in his ass, and left his body out on Forest Avenue for everyone to see. Anyway, Locke and I planned to lure Jesse to the meat packing plant on the premise of a meeting, and clipping him once we got there.

We all piled into Locke's Lincoln and rode over. Jesse drove with Frito riding shotgun, while Locke and me were in the backseat. Locke and I exchanged sinister looks as we slyly checked our weapons out of Jesse's eye sight. Frito made small talk, cracking jokes on the way over. He had us rolling.

"I got another, check it out. A lady was at

her doctor's office getting a physical. The doctor said, you're overweight and you need to lose about twenty pounds. The lady said, I want a second opinion. So the doctor said, okay, you ugly too," Frito joked once again.

We laughed as Jesse pulled into the parking lot. Jesse hopped out the car first and said, "I hope this is not going to take long. I think that bitch at the Raven was just about to give me some head."

"That cockeyed chick!" Frito asked, "You can't tell if she was looking at you or Neil," he joked as we all cracked up laughing again.

Frito opened the door and led the way into the building. Jesse was behind him. I was behind Jesse, and Locke was behind me. I reached into my waistband and pulled out my pistol ready to put a round in the back of his head, when I felt a hit to the back of my head and suddenly everything went black.

A splash of cold water hit my face violently. Confused and completely disoriented, I opened my eyes, but things were still blurry. I tried to wipe them, but I couldn't move my hands. As I began to regain my wits, I realized that I was tied up and hanging from the same hook the meat packers used to hang their beef from.

"Rise and shine slick!"

I recognized the voice as soon as I heard it.

My eyes finally came into focus and I could see Locke standing in front of me holding an empty bucket. Jesse was standing next to him, and Frito was standing behind him.

"What the hell is going on?" I snapped, "Get me down!"

Locke sat down the bucket and slowly walked over toward me, "I guess by now you can tell that we're not here about Jesse. I got some bad news for you slick," he said lighting a cigarette and then pausing for a second, "You are going to die. The only question is, will it be a quick death, or a long painful one. Depends on if you tell me everything I want to know."

"What the hell are you talking about? You lost your damn mind. I'm a captain! I haven't done anything! Socco is going to have your ass for this!" I blurted out.

"Who do you think sent me?" he replied sarcastically with a devilish grin, "I see those wheels in your head turning. You think it's a coincidence that you're hanging here after you refused to reveal your contact to Socco. That pissed him off."

"You lie!" I responded vehemently as I twisted and turned trying to get loose. *No way in hell could Socco ever betray me,* I thought. We were a close family with a lot of love between us; I was like a son to him and he a father to me.

"Believe whatever you want. I'll make you

this promise. Tell me who your contact is and where I can find him, and I'll kill you quick."

"I'm not gonna tell you a damn thing, you bastard!"

Locke chuckled as he pulled a knife out of his pocket and cut my shirt off. He placed the blade against my cheek and sliced me down to the bottom of my chin. I gritted my teeth and took the pain, trying my best not to give this prick the satisfaction of hearing me scream.

"I never did like your ass," Locke admitted.

Jesse walked over, rolled up his sleeves, and started pounding me in the ribs like a boxer hitting a punching bag. No matter how hard I tried to brace for the impact, every blow Jesse delivered was excruciatingly painful. It was hard to breath. After about an hour of this, Locke stepped in front of Jesse, who was exhausted and dripping with sweat.

"Who's your contact slick?"

I just gave him a cold hard stare, and finally used the time to catch my breath. I looked over at Frito, who was just standing there with his arms folded. I couldn't believe he'd stand by and do nothing.

"Tough little son of a bitch!" Locke commented taking a puff off a cigarette, "You know what I'm going to do when I get finished with you? I'm going to pay a little visit to that fine ass wife of yours. I'm going to tell her you ran off with some broad. She's going cry on my shoulder. And then, I'm going to fuck Fozie right in the ass with this big dick, on your bed, and she's going to love it. Soon, your little boy will be calling me daddy," he said laughing slapping me on my cut cheek.

"You motherfucker!" I yelled squirming, trying everything I could to get loose.

"Tell you what slick. You tell me your contact right now, and I promise when I'm fucking Fozie doggy-style, I'll make sure she closes the door so your son can't watch."

"Fuck you!" I yelled spitting him in the face.

Locke slashed me across the chest with that knife in retaliation causing me to yell out in pain for the first time. Jesse, after wiping his face off with a towel, came back over to go to work on me, drilling me in the same sore spot right around my ribs. I lost feeling in my arms from hanging so long, and began to cough up blood. After a few minutes, Locke walked over to Frito and handed him the knife.

"Take a break Jesse," Locke said patting Frito on the back.

Frito walked over next to Jesse as Locke took a seat on a stool and wiped his face with a towel. Jesse was slumped over trying to catch his breath when Frito tapped him on the shoulder and asked, "You okay buddy?" Before Jesse could open his mouth to respond, Frito covered his mouth and stabbed him in the neck.

When Locke finished wiping his face and saw Jesse falling to the floor and blood pouring out everywhere, he went for his gun that he sat on the table. Frito's big ass leaped over before he could reach it, and started stabbing Locke repeatedly yelling, "This is for Neil!"

Locke's bloody body lay lifeless on the concrete floor. Frito looked like a savage beast holding a knife covered in blood. He stood up, came over, and started cutting the rope to get me down.

"Careful with my arms, they're sore," I said as he helped me down from the hook.

"I'm sorry Neil. I had no idea that they were going to do this to you. I swear. It wasn't until you got knocked out that Locke told me what he had planned. He told me that Socco wanted me to kill you, and that if I did. He'd make me captain. I went along with it only so I could save you. So I had to wait until I got my first opportunity to make a move. You know I'm with you to the end."

After what happened, I didn't doubt Frito's loyalty or sincerity, but everyone else's I did. "I believe you," I said taking a seat and resting, "But you never heard Socco actually tell you that himself, did you?"

"No."

"Well, maybe Locke was lying, and he wanted my contact for himself," I added still refusing to believe that Socco could betray me.

"And what if Locke was telling the truth and Socco finds out what happened here? We're dead men! I say its highway time buddy," Frito said as he fished the keys from Locke's pocket and jingled them in front of me.

"No, I need to know the truth. Besides, I'm not running. Dallas is my home. My family and friends are here. I'm not going anywhere!"

"So what's our play?"

"Call Mousey and Charlie, have them get rid of these bodies and clean this mess up. I want you to talk to Clarence, feel him out. See if he knew about this. I'm going to have a chat with Nickel Willie. He's the key. I got to see where he stands. If Nick is on board, the other captains will fall in line if we have to make a move on Socco. But first, I need to check on my wife and son. We'll meet back here at noon.

"Ok."

━━◄◖∩◗►━━

That ride home had to be the longest of my life. A million things were swirling around in my head. I pulled into my driveway and hopped out of my car with my gun cocked. I looked around the house and down the block to make sure I wasn't followed, or that somebody was watching my house. I rushed inside the door to see my son in the living room playing with his toys inside his playpen.

"Daddy!" he yelled out.

I ran over, scooped him up, and hugged him like it was the very first time. Fozie came out of the bedroom. When she got into arm's length, I grabbed her by the waist and squeezed both of them tightly.

"What happened baby? Why are you bleeding, and why is your shirt all tore up?"

"I love you baby. I love both of you. You two are my heart," I said out of breath kissing her and Mathew all over their faces.

"Neil, baby, what's going on?" she asked with a look of concern on her face that I had never seen before.

"Locke tried to kill me tonight!"

"What? Why?"

I took Mathew back over to his playpen and sat him down. I walked to the hall closet to grab a towel, and then over to the kitchen sink to wet it with Fozie following right behind me breathing down my neck. I peeled off my bloody rags and wiped myself down with the towel. Leaning against the sink, I took a long, deep breath, "I think Socco ordered him too."

"What! What are you talking about Neil? My father would never do that!"

"I wouldn't tell him about Pete from New Orleans. That's who I've been getting my stuff from for the past two years."

"I don't believe it! He loves you! He's always telling me you're the son he never had. Why would he do that?"

"I don't know baby, but I'm going to find out," I said throwing the towel against the sink, "If it's true, I'm no longer safe."

"This can't be happening!" Fozie responded frantically pacing back and forth.

I grabbed Fozie by both arms to calm her down and hold her in place. Then I looked dead into her watery eyes, "If he wants me dead, I only have two choices. We pack everything right now, leave this house, this city, and all our friends behind, and hit the road. Or..."

"Don't say it, don't say it!" she yelled.

"I don't wanna lose my family. I'm not going to lose my family! Tell me what to do."

"You know what you're asking?"

"Yes, are you with me?" I said falling to one knee and hugging her around the waist. There was a long silence that seemed to last an eternity. She looked around at the house she'd spent the last year decorating, the vase on the end table, the oil paintings on the walls, the leather sofa, and finally back down at me. She tore herself away from my grasp, stormed down the hallway, and slammed the bedroom door behind her.

"Shit!" I murmured. I got up, went to the bathroom, and cleaned up. I called up my doctor and had him make a house call. An hour later, he came by and stitched me up right at the kitchen table. Of course, I swore him to secrecy, and paid him cash for services rendered.

I went back into the bathroom after the doctor left to look at his handy work. Staring at my reflection in the mirror, I thought I looked like a black *Frankenstein*. My face was bruised and slightly swollen from the beating, and my cheek was stitched up from Locke cutting me with that razor. Fozie walked up behind me and gently held me close while tenderly kissing my shoulder blade. She carefully touched the stitches on my face.

"I love you so much, baby. I'm with you always. Do what you have to," she replied before giving me a kiss. With shoulders slumped, she walked back to the bedroom and closed the door.

Exhausted, I laid down on the couch wanting to sleep but couldn't. I had too much on my mind for me to shut my eyes for one minute. Unable to relax, I put on my favorite Miles Davis album, *In a Silent Way.* The same one my father bought me in sixty-nine. I like to unwind or meditate to it. Lying on the couch, with my shotgun on my chest cocked and ready to go, I just stared at the clock until the sun peaked through the living room window. My mind was constantly turning. I know Frito and my wife are on my side, but who else can I trust. By the end of the day, I'll have my answers.

CHAPTER 27

MARCH 16, 1978

Once the sun was up, I drove over to Nickel Willie's house to confront him. Nick had a nice house in Oak Cliff next to the VA Hospital. It was a quiet neighborhood; most of the people that lived on his block were retirees. As I pulled up and hopped out of my car, I saw Nick on the front porch sitting in a rocking chair drinking tea from a mason jar. Nick was in bad shape at this time. He looked very frail. Doctors diagnosed him with throat cancer a couple of months back. His voice was almost gone by this point; he could barely speak above a whisper anymore. But he still got up every morning and handled his business like a true professional. And he was still highly respected. That's why his stance was so important to my future.

"Morning Nick," I said stepping up on his porch.

"Neil," he responded slowly rising to his feet. I quickly moved closer to help him up, and when I did, he gave me an unexpected hug, "I didn't think I'd see you again. Have a seat."

"How are feeling?"

"I just saw the doctor yesterday. He says I got a month or two to live," Nick said shrugging his shoulder before he started to cough violently.

"I don't understand, what happened? I thought they had good treatment for you?"

"I never took any treatment kid. I wasn't about to let them shoot that toxic shit inside of me. It would've just been prolonging the inevitable. Besides, I'm seventy four years old; I've done everything you can do in this life. I've been rich. I've been poor. I've made love to the most beautiful women. I've traveled. I have a wonderful family that I worked hard to make sure they would be well taken care of when I'm gone. There's really nothing left for me to do in this life. To be honest with you, I never thought I'd live this long."

"Have you thought about the moment, you know?"

"I try not to," Nick said before coughing again, "You know I never told anybody this, but when I go to sleep at night, I see the faces of all the men I've killed. They have no eyes, yet they're staring at me. Sounds weird, I know. They tell me they're in hell waiting on me. That's why I never sleep more than a couple of hours a night."

I shook my head, and then I changed the subject, "You know why I'm here?"

"I might be sick, but I'm still as sharp as a

razor kid," he said pointing at his head slightly covered in gray hair.

"Locke tried to kill me last night."

"Yeah, looks like they roughed you up pretty good," Nick said checking out my face, "Locke is good at pimping women, but lucky for you, he's bad at doing hits."

"I got to know, did Socco order him to do it?"

"He did. I advised him against that, but he decided to do it anyway. He's the boss."

"That motherfucker!" I yelled punching the palm of my right hand, "Why would he do that?"

"You'll have to ask him that."

"I plan to," I said looking out at the horizon as the sun was fighting its way through the morning dew. I turned back around and sat down next to Nick, "Look ah, Socco has put me in a bad spot here. It's either him or me. I really need to know where you stand."

"That's not what you want know. What you really want to know is, if you take out Socco, would I be on board? Right?"

"I guess nothing gets by you, Nick?"

"I told you I'm still sharp as a razor," he said with a devilish grin, "I thought Socco was wrong to take you out. It was an abuse of power on his part. You're a tremendous asset. You're smart. You've always shown respect and you're a damn good earner. You'll also make a great boss. Of course, I'll back you," he commented patting me on the back.

"No, I couldn't step over you and be boss. You're next in line. It's only right."

"Neil, my time is short; I don't want to spend my last days in a stressful position. It's your time my friend. Congratulations," Nick said as he slowly stood up and gave me a hug.

"Thanks."

"Let me offer you a little advice my friend. The guys you'll be leading respect two things, death and money, and not necessarily in that order. The threat of being killed will help to keep guys in line, but the ability to earn money is what will keep the men loyal to you. Never forget that."

―――

So after my meeting with Nick I went back to the plant to meet up with my crew. Frito, Mousey, and Charlie had cleaned up those dead bodies and were sitting around drinking whiskey from a brown paper bag. They all hopped to their feet when they saw me walk into the room.

"You okay boss?" Charlie asked, as they all walked over to check me out.

"I'll live."

Frito stepped closer. Smiling, he examined my stitches closely, "Very nice," he added playfully slapping me on the one spot on my jaw that didn't hurt. "Well I talked to Clarence, and he didn't know shit. He's still expecting you to show up at Benny's tonight for dinner and discuss that new nightclub you guys are opening."

"Good. I spoke to Nickel Willie...it's true. Socco ordered the hit."

"Damn! We're fucked!" Frito blurted out punching the wall.

"No we're not, because he's on board with us taking out Socco."

"So he's taking over as the boss?" Mousey asked.

"No, he's too sick for that. I'm taking over. Nick is going to stay on as my second in command. His continuing presence will give us validity. Frito will take over for me as captain, and I'm making Charlie a member," I stated with authority. The guys were stunned as they looked at each other bewilderedly. I guess the news caught them off guard. "But first things first, we got to take out Socco," I added.

"Socco is well insulated. He's going to be incredibly hard to get to. So how exactly are we going to do that?" Frito asked.

"He has one weakness, his mistress Linda. When he visits her, that's when he is most vulnerable. So here's the plan............"

Linda lived in this shotgun style frame house off Second Avenue in South Dallas. Parking on the next street over, we crept down the alley almost being exposed by all the barking dogs. Sneaking in between the houses, we could see Socco's new Cadillac parked in front of Linda's front door. The driver was sitting behind the wheel reading a magazine. The sun was setting casting a shadow over us as we leaned against this vacant house that was a couple of doors down.

"Ok Mousey, you know what to do," I whispered.

Nodding his head, Mousey grabbed a small potato we picked up at the store on the way over and put it over the barrel of his thirty-eight revolver. It was a crude, but effective, old school way to muffle the sound of his pistol. Mousey circled around the building toward the intersection with the gun hidden under his shirt. Then, he walked up the block toward the Cadillac parked on the curb. Whistling and acting carefree, Mousey pretended to be surprised when he saw Stan, the driver, in the front seat.

"Hey Stan, what's happening brother?" Mousey asked with this huge grin as walked over to the driver-side door with the gun in his left hand hidden behind his back.

"Mousey," Stan answered dropping his magazine.

"What are you doing hanging out here my man?"

"I'm driving for Socco today," Stan answered, and then he leaned a little closer, "He's in the house with that bitch Linda."

They both chuckled.

"Yeah, I got to collect from a guy down the street," Mousey said sighing, "What you reading?"

"Just checking out the latest edition of Ebony," Stan replied turning to grab the magazine he'd just tossed into the passenger seat. With his head turned, Mousey put his gun to the back of his head and pulled the trigger. It was almost instantaneous how the blood splattered against the windshield. Mousey opened the door, pushed Stan's dead body into the passenger seat, and quickly wiped the blood off the window. After he finished, he picked up Stan's magazine and pretended to read it.

With Charlie in my car with the engine running, just in case we needed to make a quick getaway, Frito and I sprinted across the street. Taking my position on the side of the front door so that I couldn't be seen through the peephole, Frito straightened the tie on his suit and rang the doorbell.

"Who is it?"

"Jehovah's Witness," Frito answered

pleasantly standing directly in front of the peep-hole flashing a smile so that she could clearly see him. Frito was just the guy to pull off this little ruse. With his chubby, freckled filled face, Frito looked more like an usher holding a collection plate at Sunday morning church service, than a ruthless gangster who could kill you in a heartbeat.

I could hear the chain being removed and the deadbolt clicking. The door creaked open, and Linda stepped out on the front porch holding her housecoat shut. Although she was dressed like she just woke up, her makeup was flawless, and her brown shoulder-length hair cascaded down her back like if it was a fine silk scarf. At twenty-seven, Linda was more than twenty years younger than Socco. He liked them young, athletic, and beautiful, and Linda was all the above, the antitheists of Aunt Anita. The adorable smile she was wearing when she poked her head out the door made me hate what we had to do.

"Good morning ma'am. Just out in your neighborhood passing out a little information," Frito said as he took a big sniff. Judging by the sweet scent of sex in the air, you can guess what was going on inside.

"I'm kind of busy at the moment. Why don't you come back later," She replied, as I slipped behind her, grabbed her around the waist with one arm, and covered her mouth with my other free hand.

Frito swiftly pulled out his gun and pointed it at her forehead, "Make a sound and I'll personally arrange a meeting with you and Jehovah right now. Nod if you understand?"

She looked at Frito with her green eyes and nodded her head.

"Everything okay?" we heard Socco yell from the bedroom.

I took my hand away from Linda's mouth. Her eyes darted back and forth between Frito and me. She stayed mute until Frito pushed the barrel of his gun against her forehead and urged her, "Say everything is fine," Frito whispered.

"It was nothing, just Jehovah Witness at the door," she yelled back.

Frito took her out to the car with Mousey. I went into the house closing the door behind me. With my pistol in hand, I eased my way down the dark hallway. I could faintly hear the sound of jazz music coming from one of the rooms. Sounded like David Brubeck's *Take Five*. I followed the music to the last room at the end of the hall, so I assumed Socco was in there. I could see the lights were on from the crack under the door. I gently opened the door and saw Socco with his back to me stripping down to his underwear.

"Come on back to bed baby!" Socco said.

"She's tied up at the moment," I replied walking in the room closing the door behind me. I stood at the foot of the bed with my weapon in hand.

Socco's head whipped around, "Neil!"

"Surprised to see me still alive?"

"What are you talking about? What happened to your face? And what are you doing here?" Socco asked with this ambiguous look, like he had no idea on earth what I was talking about.

"I'm talking about you sending Locke to kill me! And don't deny it. I already talked to Nick. I know everything."

Socco's eyes quickly focused on his gun that was sitting on the nightstand. He lunged for it, but I squeezed off a round and hit the lamp that was sitting there also. Startled, Socco recoiled and threw his hands up. "Ok, ok," Socco replied taking a deep breath and sitting down on the edge of the bed.

"Why, why did you try to have me killed? I thought I was family! I thought I was the son you never had! I thought I was the future of this family!" I yelled as I stepped closer with my gun still aimed at his head.

"You defied me, twice! I'm the boss of this family; you should've revealed your contact to me when I asked."

"So this was all about fucking money? I gave

you your cut and then some, just like I was sup-posed to."

"It wasn't just about the money; it was also about the fact that you broke a sacred rule, Neil. When the boss gives you an order, you follow it. No exceptions! If I let you slide, the next guy will be doing the same thing. Give a man an inch, he'll take a mile. No way was I about to allow that to happen."

"Wasn't it you that taught me that a man's word is everything. That's all I was doing, keep-ing my word."

"I also taught you to remember your oath, to put the interest of this family above all others, to follow the orders of the boss, me."

"Bullshit! If this was just about a sacred rule, why have me tortured? Look at my face Socco. Look at my fucking face! Locke beat the hell out of me trying to make me give up my contact. So don't give me that bullshit, cause this is all about money!"

"And what if is? Still doesn't change anything. I'm the boss. I gave you an order, and you're sup-posed to follow it, period," Socco stated boldly as he bowed his head and cleared his throat. "Look Neil, I love you. I truly do. You are the son I never had. Yeah I admit part of my decision was based on money. I thought I could make more money with that contact than you. But the major part is your refusal to tell me. I don't see why you're so surprised. You knew the rules and the possible consequences when you became a part of this thing. And there's only one thing you can be certain of, we're all going to hell."

"So where does that leave us?"

"Why do you ask questions you already know the answers to," Socco replied as he stood up and locked eyes with me, "Do what you came here to do! I'm ready. Shit, I'm surprised I lived this long."

My hand began to tremble a little for the first time. The tears were forming in my eyes. Socco meant everything to me. I loved him. His influence on my life was immeasurable.

"I'll make it easy for you," Socco said turning around so that I didn't have to look at his face, "Just do me a small favor. I know you're going to do right by my daughter. Just make sure that your Aunt Anita is taken care of, okay?"

"I will," I replied gathering myself, and putting my emotions aside to do what needed to be done. I gripped my gun tighter, focused on the back of his head, and squeezed the trigger. Socco's brains splattered against the wall as his body dropped like a wet rag. I wiped the tears from my eyes, stood over the top of his body, and fired several more times. I didn't want to take any chances.

Dropping my gun on the floor, I took a deep breath and sat down on the edge of the bed. My mind started swirling with questions. How am I going to clean up this mess? How am I going to break this news to Aunt Anita? How am I going to tell the family? What am I going to do about Linda? Should I tell Fozie the truth about what happened here? Then it hit me like a ton of bricks. I'M THE BOSS. I'M THE BOSS. *Wow* I thought. The torch was officially passed. Then, just like that, my whole mentality changed. My focused changed. Things became crystal-clear to me. Everything that Socco and Nick taught me about the game over the years, suddenly made sense.

Rising to my feet, I grabbed my gun off the floor and stuck it in my waistband. I walked back to the front door and signaled for Frito and Mousey to come back in. Frito had his gun pressed against Linda's head as he led her back in with Mousey following.

"So what are we going to do with her?" Mousey asked checking the street one last time before closing the door behind him.

"We could always use a patsy," Frito urged.

"Don't kill me Neil! Please don't kill me. You know me, you know I won't say anything, I swear to God," Linda begged falling to her knees.

I looked into her pleading eyes and said,

"Sorry Linda. You fucked with the wrong man."

I gave the nod to Frito, and he shot her in the temple. Frito wiped his fingerprints off the gun and placed it Linda's hand. We arranged the scene to make it look like a murder suicide.

As word of what happened in Linda's house started spreading through the streets of South Dallas, I had Nickel Willie call an emergency meeting that evening. Normally, it would be at Roscoe's, but with Socco dead, and the family being under a watchful eye of the law, Nick thought it would be better to meet in the garage at his auto shop. As the guys started showing up one by one, I could feel the tension in the room growing. Staring at my face, I could hear the whispers as Nick finally raised his hand and the room fell silent. He'd been sipping on herbal tea with honey in it to try to get as much power in his voice as humanly possible.

"Gentlemen, is everyone here?" Nick asked.

"Locke! Locke is missing!" several voices yelled from the crowd.

"By know you've probably all heard what happened to Socco. Apparently, he was shot by some crazy woman he was seeing. A tragedy to say the least," Nick struggled to say as the heads in the crowd nodded in agreement.

"But we also had another incident. Neil," Nick said calling me over, and putting his arm around my shoulder. For the occasion, I had put on my best custom-made silk suit, gray with a black shirt and a black and gray tie, "Was attacked by Locke without cause. Our friend barely escaped with his life. When we find Locke, he will have to answer for this."

Many in the crowd shared the same bewildered expression upon hearing the news about Locke. They were shaking their heads in total disbelief, but none would challenge the information since it was coming from the highly respected Nickel Willie.

"With Socco gone, it's obvious we need new leadership. Normally, since I'm second in charge, I would naturally take over. But as you all know, I've been ill, and having the stress of running this family is a burden I don't need right now. So, I know that if Socco were here, he would want his trusted and loyal son-in-law, Neil to take over as boss. The rules say we must take a vote on it. So I nominate Neil as the next boss, a show of hands for all that agrees," Nick commanded raising his own hand first.

This was really just a formality. I was going to be the boss no matter what. But the one thing this vote did was reveal if there was any dissention among the ranks. So I watched carefully as the guys raised their hands in agreement one by one. The last to raise his hand was Clarence. Hesitating momentarily, Clarence gazed at my face one last time before he threw his hand up in agreement. I walked over, stood in front of the entire crew, and was greeted with thunderous applause.

"Thank you. This is a difficult time for us. Losing Socco hurts. He meant a lot to me, and I know how much he meant to each of you. He will be missed. But make no mistake; we will survive. We will move on. Business will continue. Our future is bright, and we'll come out of this tragedy stronger than ever," I stated with authority as I received another thunderous applause.

———

After settling things with that family, now I have to go and deal with my other family. I pulled into Socco's driveway just as the sun was setting. I noticed Fozie's car parked out front as I slowly made my way up the steps. I closed my eyes, took a deep breath, and rang the doorbell. Fozie opened the door, dabbing her tear-stained eyes with tissue. Sitting on the couch holding a box of Kleenex, crying her eyes out, was Anita.

"Neil, oh my God!" Anita yelled running over and squeezing me tight, "They just called and told me that Socco is dead. Shot in the head. What the hell happened?"

"I hate to tell you this, but Socco had been seeing this woman, Linda, for some time. I found out through my sources at the police department that she shot him and then shot herself," I replied patting her on the back.

"I knew Socco had a little fling going on, but nothing like this."

"Yeah, I hate to be the bearer of bad news; I know how much you loved him. He told me that he was ending it. Maybe that's what happened?" I said shrugging my shoulders.

"No, no no no," Anita yelled as she broke down even more and ran to the bathroom slamming the door behind her.

Fozie walked over toward me with this solemn look on her face and whispered, "What really happened Neil?"

"That is what happened baby."

"C'mon Neil, don't bullshit me. I know you were planning to confront him. I just want the truth."

I thought about it for a moment. Would telling her the truth make any difference? Would knowing the truth bring her any comfort? Hell no. Socco was her father. She loved him, and deep down inside; she didn't really want to know the truth about him. So I told her what she wanted to hear.

"I was on my way over there to confront him,

but when we arrived, he was already dead. I'm so sorry baby," I explained.

Fozie looked at me with this perplexed expression. I think deep down in her heart, she was looking for a reason to believe me. It took a moment for her to digest it, but she eventually did. She never asked me another question about it, and we never discussed this situation ever again. I would take this secret to the grave. She collapsed in my arms like a runner who just finished a marathon. I held her tightly and caressed the back of her head, soothing her pain away the best that I could.

66 There is really nothing more to tell sister. Nick passed away that summer of cancer, and I made sure that Clarence had an unfortunate accident. With those two gone, I plugged in soldiers that were loyal to me and pushed on. I did as promised, and took care of Anita until she passed away a couple of years ago. Life has been pretty much routine after that. I am the boss, and I run my family. I get up and go to work every morning, just like your average working class man. I never personally killed another person after that. Of course, through the years I still had to order the death of many. I guess I could list them all if you need me to?" my father asked.

"That won't be necessary," Sister Simmons replied shaking her head.

"Well, these days I just enjoy spending time with my wife and family. I've been happily married to Fozie now for thirty-two years. The only woman I had ever been with. The only woman I ever loved," my father said turning toward Sister Simmons and smiling, "You already met our son Mathew. He's given me two wonderful grandkids, Desmond and Naomi. Things had been simple right up until the day I was shot."

"I'm so sorry Neil. This should have never happened to you."

"It's not your fault sister. Shit happens. You play the hand your dealt."

"It is my fault. I should have been there for you."

"What are you talking about sister?"

Sister Simmons walked over to the sink, turned on the faucet, and wet a paper towel. Wiping her face, the elderly lady walked over toward the window, cracked the curtains, and looked out on the Dallas skyline.

"Neil I eh...I," she mumbled searching for the right words. She turned and faced my father. Walking over toward him, she took off her white veil and placed it on the table, "Look at me Neil. Look at my face."

My father wiped the matter out of his eyes and focused as hard as he could on Sister Simmons' face, "Okay."

"Neil...my first name is Estelle. Simmons is my maiden name. When I was married and living in New York City, my last name was Wright, the same as my husband...Raymond."

"WHAT!" my father blurted out, as his eyes almost popped out of his head.

"I know it's been a long time since the last

time you saw me, but it's me Neil, your mother," Sister Simmons stated with tear stained eyes.

"Momma?"

"Yes."

"Where the hell happened to you?" my father snapped, "Why did you never come back for me."

"After my mother and father died. I lost it Neil. I turned into an alcoholic and lost everything. I wrongly blamed your father and I went back to Carolina, where things only got worst. I got hooked on drugs and was homeless living on the streets. It wasn't until I got arrested for stealing, and got two years in prison, that I finally got cleaned up. Thanks to a very special priest, I was delivered from those demons. I got on my feet and gave my life to Christ. By the time that happened and I walked out of prison, ten years had passed and it was 79. I went back to New York and tried to look for you and your father, but all anyone could tell me was that ya'll went to Texas. I thought I lost you forever. I decided to dedicate my life to helping others. To try to make up for all the damage I've done," Sister Simmons revealed rubbing my father's arm, "I love you so much Neil. I never meant to hurt you baby. I hope you can find it in your heart to forgive me son."

With tears pouring from his eyes, he turned and looked away. She leaned over, pushed some of his IV lines and tubes to the side, and gave him the sweetest, longest, most tender hug that a mother can give her son. Then she stood up and pulled off a necklace with a heart shaped locket.

"You and you father were always close to my heart son," she stammered out, opening the locket to reveal an old black and white picture of the three of them.

My father took the necklace in his hands and looked at the picture with his mouth open. Closing his eyes, he held the necklace close to his heart. "I hated the fact that you left for a long time momma, but I have to be honest. I never stopped loving you. I never stopped looking for you. I never stopped wondering what happened to you. I never stopped wondering if you were okay every day of my life since you left," he said smiling, despite the pain.

"You never have to wonder again baby, because I'm here to stay," she responded smiling, kissing my father all over his face. Barely able to tear herself away, Sister Simmons walked over to her black bag and pulled out her Bible, "Neil, it's my fault that those horrible things happened to you. All you ever wanted was love, and a family of your own. And if I had never left, I don't think your life would have turned out the way it did. Let me help you now. Let me try to save you. Will you pray with me?"

My old man wiped the tears from his eyes, and nodded his head yes.

Sister Simmons cracked opened her Bible and turned to Romans 10:9, "If thou shalt confess with thy mouth the Lord Jesus and shalt believe in thine heart that God has raised him from the dead. Thou shalt be saved," she read, and then pulled out an old prayer card wedged in between the pages. She turned to my father and asked him, "Neil, do you believe in God?"

"Yes I do."

"Then I want you to repeat after me."

"Okay."

"Heavenly Father, have mercy on me, a sinner. I believe in you and that your word is true. I believe that Jesus Christ is the son of the living God and that he died on the cross so that I may now have forgiveness for my sins and eternal life. I know that without you in my heart my life is meaningless.

I believe in my heart that you, Lord God, raised Him from the dead. Please Jesus forgive me, for every sin I have ever committed or done in my heart, please Lord Jesus forgive me and come into my heart as my personal Lord and Savior today. I need you to be my Father and my friend.

I give you my life and ask you to take full control from this moment on; I pray this in the name of Jesus Christ, Amen."

My father repeated what she said, word-for-word. He closed his eyes, clutched his heart, and let out a deep sigh, like the weight of the world was pulled off his shoulders. Sister Simmons came back over and gave him another hug.

"Praise God!" she blurted out.

Just then, the door opened, and a tall, lanky brother wearing scrubs and a white lab coat came strolling in. Looking down the hallway behind him one last time, he quickly shut the door.

"Hate to break up this love fest, but our patient needs some more medicine," the brother said taking the cap off a syringe.

"I thought I said I didn't want to be disturbed. Where is Earl?" my father stated.

"I'm sorry, but I had to ask your friends to leave. They were interfering with hospital staff," the brother said walking over to my father's bedside and carefully injecting the old man's IV bag.

"Wait a minute, who are you? And where's the other doctor who was in here earlier?"

"He's tied up at the moment," the brother said with a sinister smile, "Don't worry, this will only take a minute."

"Who are you and what are you giving me?" my father asked again.

"Neil, you don't remember me," the brother asked sarcastically, "Let me see if I can refresh your memory."

Tossing the syringe in the trash, he opened up his lab coat, and pulled down his pants and underwear around his knees. Sister Simmons gasped and turned her head at the site, and my father's jaw nearly hit the floor. The man had no penis, only a plastic tube in the place where it would be located. My father looked at his face, and it hit him.

"Mark!"

"That's right, and I've been waiting a long time for this. I tried to get you earlier."

"It was you at the warehouse!"

"Yep, and this time, I'm going to finish the job. I just gave you a lethal dose of fentanyl. You'll be dead in ten minutes," he said pulling his pants back up.

"You didn't have to do this young man. My son just gave his life to God," Sister Simmons interjected crying. She scrambled to her feet trying to make it to the door to get help, but Mark pushed her down in the chair next to the bed.

"I don't give a damn! Your son cut my dick off lady! He ruined my life! I never had kids! Never got married! What woman would want me? Only satisfaction I have, is watching your son die!" he screamed.

"It's okay mom," my father said holding her hand, "I love you, and you saved me. That's all that counts. Mark," he said locking eyes with him, "I'm sorry for hurting you. I hope you find your peace. I've finally found mine," my father said totally at easy with the situation.

He started having trouble breathing and his eyes rolled back into his head. Mark stumbled backwards, pushed opened the door, and sprinted down the hall. He almost knocked me over as my mother, my wife, and my kids walked into the room to greet him. We were horrified to find my father going into convulsions. Sister Simmons scrambled to find the call button and signal the real hospital staff. They rushed in and performed CPR, but despite their best efforts, he died from the over dose.

Once the chaos finally calmed down, I pulled Sister Simmons to the side and had her tell me everything, the whole conversation, every single detail. That day I lost my father. My children lost their grandfather. But we gained a grandmother we never knew, and through her, we found our long lost connection to the past. I could even see a little of my father in her face, guess that's why she looked so familiar to me. As a result, we became a closer family. Through tragedy, we found strength in each other. My father's life and death were not in vain.

So like I said at the beginning, I'm sitting here with the daunting task of writing my father's obituary. And now that you have soaked it all in, like I have, what do you think? Is Neil Wright just some crazy sociopath, and the world is a better place now that he's dead? Or is he a good-hearted man who was dealt a lousy hand in life, and made many poor choices. I guess I've come to the realization. It doesn't matter. All that matters in the end; is that he loved us and was there for us, and that he got himself right with God. I believe he's in heaven now looking down on me. A comforting thought that warms my heart.

I look forward to getting to know the grandmother I never knew. I never saw a woman so happy in my life. She stayed at my house every night since my father passed. She spent countless hours telling my wife, my kids, and me all about our entire family history. It should have been a sad time for us, but it wasn't. Night after night, we sat on the floor in living room browsing through the numerous pictures she had of my father, grandfather, cousins, and great-grandparents. It was a bittersweet time. I wish my father was there to enjoy it with us.

The police finally found Frito yesterday. Mark had shot him, and Frito had stumbled into a wooded area next to that old warehouse where he bled out. My father's two bodyguards are loyal, tough, but not too bright. They found themselves in an early grave for allowing my father to be killed.

Oh, one last thing. Don't think for one moment I've forgotten about Mark. With my father's passing, the torch has been officially handed to me. Now I'm the boss. And with my new authority, I sent my guys to find Mark. My father may have been at peace, but no way was I going to let that shit slide. I had my guys make sure that Mark had himself a little accident. When they caught up with him, they drenched him with lighter fluid, set him on fire, and threw him fifty stories from the observation deck of a downtown skyscraper. Oh well, I guess you'll have to pray for me, because I'm not there yet. After all, I am my father's son.

THE END

ALSO BY OMAR SCOTT

THE HANDS OF LOVE

Lorenzo Love, or Ren as he's known on the streets, is not your typical veteran detective. He's a smooth-talking, streetwise brother who is quite cunning. He cleverly juggles his home life, which includes his young son and loving wife, a needy mistress, and a narcotics unit of dirty cops that have been taking money under the table from dangerous drug-dealers. Ren has always been crafty at maneuvering his way out of difficult situations. But now his "bad-boy" ways are finally catching up with him. His relationship with his mistress is unraveling, Internal Affairs is investigating his crew for an illegal shooting, and a string of young ladies are brutally murdered one by one with the evidence pointing directly at Ren. The race is on to cover his tracks, clear his crew, and find a serial killer before it's too late. Can Ren slip out of another tight squeeze, or will he finally go down? The Hands of Love is a fast paced well-crafted novel weaving its way through the crime-infested streets of East Dallas. This intense thriller will have your eyes glued to every page right up to the unbelievable ending.

Learn more at:
www.outskirtspress.com/thehandsoflove